Stretched across the couch was a tall human-looking man with dark hair, massive black wings and dressed all in black velvet. He was gorgeous, rock god gorgeous. Dangerous gorgeous. In one hand was a wine glass and he gestured to an attendant for more wine. The servant had a human body with a hound's head, he looked familiar and my mind started working trying to figure out from where.

"Aah, I see you made it back. Have you learned your lesson?" asked the man on the chaise.

"Yes, my Lord. But I have a problem," said my guide.

"Yes, I can see that." He looked down his nose at me.

"She of whom we cannot speak trapped me in a mirror."

The man on the couch laughed. "You fell for that? I'm ashamed of you."

"This girl released me," Archimedes pointed at me. "But I'm not powerful enough to undo the magic which now affects her."

"Release the girl," said the winged guy to Archimedes. He moved toward us almost sliding across the floor; it looked that effortless.

Archimedes let go of my arm and I collapsed to the floor. The room spun in circles. As the head honcho came over, I noticed he had small, black horns on his head. Who was this guy?

"Yes, I see. She is quite tasty isn't she? You do have a soft spot for women, don't you?"

Archimedes put his head down, looking sheepish.

"Now, wait a minute. I helped him, now he's going to help me and then I go home."

# INFECTED BY MAGIC

# ALSO BY LINDA JORDAN

*The Jeweled World Series:*

*The Black Opal: Book 1*

*The Enigmatic Pearl: Book 2*

*The Flaming Ruby: Book 3*

*(Series Complete with Book 3)*

*Elemental: 5 Stories for Teens*

*Stories of the Jeweled Worlds*

*Faerie Unraveled: The Bones of the Earth Series, Book 1*

# INFECTED BY MAGIC

LINDA JORDAN

METAMORPHOSIS PRESS

Published by Metamorphosis Press

www.metamorphosispress.com

*ISBN 13:978-0997797190*

*To Michael and Zoe ~*
*for patience beyond belief*

# CHAPTER ONE

I STOMPED DOWN FIFTEENTH AVE. My fists clenched, sweat made my T-shirt stick, but I kept going, my Docs pounding the sidewalk. Rage pooled in the shadows of huge trees. So mad at Mom, the world and myself. Mostly myself.

We got into it again before she left for her meeting. She yelled at me for not being ambitious enough, not having a clue what I wanted to do with my life and not wanting to go to camp or school this summer. I yelled at her for working so much and moving to stupid Seattle.

I hated the city with its gray, moldy days. I just wanted to go back to the sticks in Eastern Washington where it's hot and I could be really alone, but I didn't want to live with Dad. Ever since the accident he's hated me as much as I hated myself. Mom, at least tolerated me.

Both Mom and I knew none of that was the real issue. The real problem was that two years ago my brother died. I loved him. Worshipped him, really. He was the golden boy. He was sixteen and I was fourteen. Chris was great at any sport, got good grades and everyone loved him.

I was just the geeky loner of the family. I still am, even though there's no family left.

He was on track to finish high school early and go to UC-Davis, to study winemaking and business, then come home and take over the winery from our parents. We'd both grown up drinking wine, but he had the nose. He could tell you everything about the wine just from smelling it and one small taste. I just got buzzed.

I rounded the corner and walked past more rich houses shaded by massive maple trees. It rained yesterday so everything smelled wet and clean. Not like the dry sandy clean of Benton City, where the heat baked everything clean. I wished it could bake me clean.

After Chris died, it only took a few months for Mom and Dad's marriage to fall apart. First they split. Mom and I moved to an apartment in the Tri-cities. Then after the divorce, three weeks ago, we moved to crappy Seattle. Mom still owns half the winery, her job has always been PR. But now she's doing it on this side of the mountains for a coop of wineries she put together. Dad and I haven't spoken since the accident.

I'm sixteen now, so only a couple more years here and then Mom says I go to college somewhere, to study something. Or maybe I'll just disappear. And make a bigger mess of my life. I don't want to be anything when I grow up. I just want to undo the accident and change everything back the way it was. To have my brother back and a home again.

Stomping down the street, I saw a pile of cardboard boxes, an overstuffed, maroon chair, an old, rickety side table and a free sign. Out of one of the boxes stuck a tall, ancient mirror. The glass looked cloudy, but the dark, wood frame was intricately carved with swirls and animals.

The mirror would be interesting in my bedroom. It looked mysterious. I pulled it out of the box of books which anchored it. We'd only lived in Seattle two weeks, but apparently it was garage sale season, being the one sort of dry month of the year. Rich people gave stuff away, never thinking about selling it. Or maybe these were garage sale leftovers. The mirror was heavy and as tall as me, but I lugged it three blocks back home, sweat dripped off me as I went. We lived in a tiny, dumpy house on the edge of the rich part of Capital

Hill. It's not home. I had no home, no matter how much I wanted one, I didn't fit in anywhere, anymore.

Mom was gone by the time I got back, just as I expected. She's always at press meetings or going back to Eastern Washington to meet with other winery owners.

I wrestled the mirror through the hallway, still crowded with unpacked boxes, and into my bedroom. I'd painted it a dark, purple color - eggplant. Lined with still empty bookcases, gold and crimson gauzy material and beads and sparkly things. The old mirror fit in. I rummaged around in the laundry room, until I found the hammer and some nails to hang it. Pulling a strip of the fabric over my desk aside, I banged on the wall until I found the studs. After the nails were in, I strung some wire through the old hangers on the back of the mirror and hung it up, arranged the fabric around it. Dragged another box of books into my room and shut the door. I lit a few candles and switched on my iPod in its dock. Then I lit sandalwood incense.

Another perfect summer day, spent in the dark mystery of my room. I lay back on the velvety covers of my bed and listened to the pulsating music.The candle light flickered in the mirror and reflected off the sparkly sequins from the scarves and beads. I loved my room. It felt hypnotizing. As I drifted off to sleep I could almost imagine I saw a face in the mirror.

# CHAPTER TWO

I WOKE up to the phone ringing. Groggily, I stood and walked to the kitchen to pick it up.

"Hullo,"

"Angie, I'm not going to make it home for dinner."

"Okay." Typical Mom.

"There's stuff for salad in the fridge. Or you can order out for pizza."

"Okay, thanks."

"Are you okay?"

"Yeah."

I hadn't been okay for two years, since Chris died.

"I should be home around nine," said Mom

"Okay."

I looked at the clock. It was five. I'd slept for six hours. I'd be up all night again. I liked the nighttime. Sometimes I would sit out on the back porch and close my eyes and pretend that beyond the streetlights in the darkness lay vast stretches of sagebrush and vineyards backed by the Horse Heaven Hills.

But it was too humid, wet and gray here. I couldn't see the stars or smell the dessert. It wasn't dusty like Benton City. It was moldy. Even in the summer.

I went back to my room, turned on the light and blew out the two candles that still burned. I turned my iPod off and unpacked another box of my salvation - books. My only friends. This box had *Lord of the Rings*, *His Dark Materials* trilogy and lots of Shakespeare in it. The heavyweights, even though Shakespeare wrote a lot of fluff. While putting them on the shelves I heard a scratching sound, sort of like fingernails on a blackboard. It sent shivers through my bones. I wondered if water pipes ran under my bedroom. Or if a mouse was in the walls. I walked around trying to isolate the sound. Finally, I realized it came from the mirror.

I could see the shadow of a hand, fingernails scratched at the mirror's surface.

"What the hell?" I felt tingling on the back of my neck. This was creepy.

A quiet voice asked, "Is anyone there?"

"What is going on?" I asked, trembling.

A face appeared, swirling into form, at first an old guy, then it settled into a gorgeous man with long, dark hair.

"Who are you?"

"Help me, please."

"Who are you?" I asked again. "What are you?"

He looked puzzled, "A man of course."

"What are you doing in that mirror?"

"I was trapped here by an evil demon. Please, help me."

"How?"

"Find a dark place and break the mirror."

"And then what, I unleash all the demons from Hell with you? Is this a trick?"

He laughed, "No, I'm truly the only one in here."

"But what if this isn't your world?"

"I can find my way home, once I'm free of this enchantment. Please, haven't you ever wanted to go home? I must rescue the rest of my family."

I felt dubious. Things like this happened only in books, not in real life. Was I still asleep and dreaming? If I was, then there wouldn't be any harm in releasing him. If this was reality and I hadn't gone insane, then there might be harm.

"Please. I may already be too late."

I unhooked the mirror and stood it by the door which I shut, grabbed the hammer and turned off the light. My eyes adjusted to the darkness; the window shade let in just enough light to see outlines of large furniture. "Is this dark enough?"

"Yes, it will be perfect."

"So, all I have to do is break the glass?"

"Yes. I'll stand back."

I couldn't fathom how he could stand back inside a mirror. I gripped the wooden frame and wedged it between my Docs. Good thing I had them and jeans on. With my other hand I swung the hammer, hitting the glass. All I heard was cracking.

"Harder."

I took a deep breath and swung harder, shutting my eyes, afraid I might get glass in them. Shattering and crashing filled the room. It sounded louder than it should have for the amount of glass in the mirror.

A breeze blew through and the air became completely still. A sweet smell flittered past me and seemed to land on my skin. It felt like a million spiders crawling on me, leaving silken strands crisscrossing me.

Then I was aware of the solid presence of another body in the room. Breathing.

"Thank you, you may bring light again."

I opened the door, slightly afraid of what I'd see. I expected to see glass everywhere, but the mirror was still intact. I was pleasantly surprised. I looked at the man standing in front of me. He was maybe twenty, big brown eyes and wearing a red shirt, brown pants and boots. Really gorgeous, but in a too perfect sort of way.

He bowed at me and said, "Thank you."

Something about him bothered me. Too cocky, maybe. I turned away and looked at the mirror. "Is this thing safe now?"

"Safe? If you're asking whether anyone else will appear in it, the answer is no."

"Good. Because I really like the mirror. Now how did you end up in it? Things like this just don't happen." I set the hammer down and hung the mirror back up.

"Ah. Like I said, a demon put me into it and transported the mirror into your world."

"That doesn't makes any sense to me." I felt lightheaded and nauseous. The sweet scent still pervaded my room. Maybe it was too much incense. I started to crumple.

He caught me and helped me back to my feet. "Come, I think you need fresh air. The release of so much magic has that effect on one."

He led me out of my room and down the hallway as I tripped over the boxes and onto the wrap around front porch. It was shady and cool. The sky was overcast. I sat down on a wood bench Mom had bought.

"Breathe," he said.

I tried, but my head didn't clear.

He sat beside me, took my chin in his hands and said, "Oh dear. I didn't mean for this to happen."

"What?" I could see he looked older in the evening light. Not twenty, more like fifty. And his brown hair was gray. "What's happening?"

"This is bad. I need to get help for you."

"What is happening?" I felt panicked.

"Nothing that can't be fixed," he said.

I was beginning to get really mad at this guy jerking me around. "Listen, it's been interesting, but now it's time for you to go."

"I am going, but you'll need to come with me."

This jerk was truly amazing. I laughed.

"I see you don't believe me. Stand up."

I glared at him. I'd prove him wrong, whatever it was. I stood up and keeled over. I grabbed at the wall of the house to steady myself. The smell still surrounded me. My clothes must be imbedded with it from when the mirror broke or didn't break, whatever happened. But it didn't smell like my incense. "What's that smell?"

"It's the smell amber makes when it burns. It's the smell of magic."

"Magic."

"A nonbeliever, I see. Just because one doesn't believe in something doesn't negate its existence."

I tried to walk, but my head wouldn't clear. "What's wrong with me?"

"You've been exposed to too much magic."

I snorted. "What does that mean? It'll wear off, right?"

He laughed. "It's not like wine, my child."

"I'm not your child."

"It won't wear off. It must be removed."

"Removed? Sheesh. Okay, so remove it."

"I can't. I do not have that power. But I do know someone who does. Which is why I said you must come with me."

"Listen, you're some creepy guy who's trapped in a mirror for who knows what. I released you and now you want me to come with you? I may be a country hick, but I'm not stupid." I leaned harder against the wall, feeling burning in my belly.

"I don't mean you any harm," he said, those brown eyes had changed to silver. He pulled sunglasses out of a pocket. "It's not far."

"Where is it you want to take me?"

"My mentor is close. Just down the hill and across the canal."

"I can't walk that far," I said, feeling the world swirl around me.

"You have a bus system, I believe."

"What are you?"

"Not human, but I am in your debt and will protect you."

"Protect me from what?" Things felt unnerving.

"We must go. Time is getting short," he said, glancing toward the yard.

"I don't think I can make it to any bus stop." I didn't want to go with this guy, but my head wasn't clearing. I noticed shadows swimming at the edge of my vision. Menacing shadows which flew and crawled through the bushes. I shivered.

"I will help you." He took my arm and I felt a rush of clarity in my mind. The shadows disappeared and I could stand without falling over.

"I need to leave Mom a note."

He led me back inside. I grabbed my small bag with my cell, wallet, mace and keys and slipped it on. I managed to write Mom a note saying I was going to a movie. Don't wait up. Then struggled to get the key in the lock and locked the door.

With his help, I made it over to Broadway to the #43 line. No one else was at the stop. Trendy people wandered by going into cafes and shops, ignoring us. I sat inside at the bus stop, while he stood outside of it, a dark, ominous shadow. His presence felt like a heavy pressure on my head, which actually helped with the dizziness. The bus pulled up and he walked in first, the bus driver didn't even see him. I paid only one fare. No argument.

I sat next to him on the nearly empty bus. We were silent as the bus rolled down Capitol Hill and across the University Bridge. He nudged me and we got off on the first stop on the Ave. I felt dizzy unless he was touching me and I didn't want to touch him. Not hip to hip, his arm around me. Yech, he felt like stalker material, but somehow he was able to push the vertigo away. We got off and walked two blocks to the UW.

It was a July evening so there weren't many people around. I didn't even know if the UW had night classes in the summer. They probably did. Some doofus would want to go to school then. I'd been home schooled until high school, then Mom ran out of time for me. It happened at the same time Chris died and Mom and Dad's marriage fell apart. High school was a waste for most kids--too wrapped up in all the social crap. I just kept being a loner and did my work. Then went home to read the books I wanted to read and listen to music. I hated school.

I finally asked the mirror guy, "What's your name?"

"I can't tell you."

"Why?"

"You're human."

"And therefore untrustworthy?" I stopped walking. "Wait, and you're not human?"

He turned to me with a grin that chilled my blood.

I didn't say anything else. Clearly not human. But what was there besides human? I felt afraid and just needed to get this over with. I wanted to turn my head without feeling like my brain was swooshing around inside. The dizziness had grown worse whenever he wasn't touching me. And his touching me felt creepy. I couldn't figure out which one scared me more.

Mirror guy led me into a parking garage and in a dark corner there was a vent. He removed the vent cover and said, "This is an entrance," motioning for me to crawl inside.

"To what? The sewers?" All I could see was a gross, dark hole.

"No, they use it for pipes and wiring between buildings. It is our home at this current time."

"Who is 'our'?" Was this guy homeless?

"Please. Go in. Before someone comes. You need to have the magic removed from you or you'll continue to deteriorate."

"You haven't told me why you were in the mirror."

"Nor will I. Are you going in or shall I leave you here?"

I didn't trust him, but whenever he let go of me the entire world reeled and my last meal threaten to come back up. So, I crawled into the dusty vent thinking I must be crazy.

He followed me and pulled the vent cover back on. The tunnel was large enough that I let him pass by me and go first. After a short time we could stand up. He pulled something out of his pocket, it looked like a stone. It lit up and I could see about as well as by flashlight. After a time we came to some pipes and from beneath them he pulled out a torch. He blew and it caught fire. It cast more light than the stone, which he slipped into his pocket again. Clearly whoever he was, he used totally different technology than I did. Glowing stones and torches that lit when you blew on them. I wasn't in Kansas anymore, Toto.

The tunnels we went through were dusty. It smelled like an old deserted concrete building. At first it felt chilly in a damp sort of way. Gray concrete walls. On one side ran pipes and electrical cables as thick as my calves. Warm pipes. We went down two levels and it got hotter. Some of the tunnels were just tall enough to walk upright in, others large enough to drive a semi through. There must have been miles of tunnels down here, crisscrossing the entire campus.

"Do you actually know where you're going?" I finally asked.

"Yes," he said. "But I must make certain we're not being followed."

I looked behind us. "Who could possibly be following us."

"There are creatures who would love to find our destination."

"What creatures and what destination?" This was all so unreal. It creeped me out, I rubbed the goosebumps on my arms.

"Just creatures, for now. I am taking you to someone who can remove the magic which is infecting you."

"And who is this someone."

"This is not a safe place to say his name."

I ground my teeth together. This guy was really annoying. If he hadn't been keeping the dizziness at bay, I'd have been gone a long time ago.

Finally he stopped on the third level down. We were in a large room. He stood by one wall and whispered to it. Then backed away and waited. The wall grew transparent and an open doorway appeared. The crawly skin spiders returned and I shivered.

He led us through. The doorway vanished and become wall again. Two huge gargoyles sat on each side of us. Except they were alive. Red eyes stared at us and I felt like they'd just as soon eat me as look at me. I shuddered as we continued down a hallway covered with shiny, red and black tiles on the floor, ceiling and walls.

I ran my hand along the wall, steadying myself, and felt the cool smoothness. Torches stuck in holders on the walls caused flames to dance across the glossy tiles. The dusty smell was gone, replaced by the unexplained scent of lemons. This place was beautiful and eerie at the same time. It sure wasn't part of the UW. Where was I?

My guide, who I'd dubbed Archimedes since he wouldn't tell me his name, stuck the torch into an empty holder on the wall. A reddish glow permeated everything. We entered a huge room with large cushions scattered about on the floor. Some were occupied by human looking creatures, others not so human, drinking and eating and partying. There was a raised area at one end with a fancy couch on it, a chaise lounge. All the furnishings were red or gold colored, just like everyone's clothing. It looked like a place that should have been filled with cigarette smoke, but the air smelled fresh and clean.

Stretched across the couch was a tall human-looking man with dark hair, massive black wings and dressed all in black velvet. He was gorgeous, rock god gorgeous. Dangerous gorgeous. In one hand was a wine glass and he gestured to an attendant for more wine. The servant had a human body with a hound's head, he looked familiar and my mind started working trying to figure out from where.

"Aah, I see you made it back. Have you learned your lesson?" asked the man on the chaise.

"Yes, my Lord. But I have a problem," said my guide.

"Yes, I can see that." He looked down his nose at me.

"She of whom we cannot speak trapped me in a mirror."

The man on the couch laughed. "You fell for that? I'm ashamed of you."

"This girl released me," Archimedes pointed at me. "But I'm not powerful enough to undo the magic which now affects her."

"Release the girl," said the winged guy to Archimedes. He moved toward us almost sliding across the floor; it looked that effortless.

Archimedes let go of my arm and I collapsed to the floor. The room spun in circles. As the head honcho came over, I noticed he had small, black horns on his head. Who was this guy?

"Yes, I see. She is quite tasty isn't she? You do have a soft spot for women, don't you?"

Archimedes put his head down, looking sheepish.

"Now, wait a minute. I helped him, now he's going to help me and then I go home." I felt nervous. This whole thing was bizarre. I must be dreaming, but I'd bloody well stand up for myself, even if it was a dream.

"Ah, so you do speak? Well, I think you won't be leaving us that quickly. I need to study you to see how deep the infection goes. I'm not sure I can undo it."

"What infection?"

"You've been infected by very powerful magic, my child. Now, if it was my own, I could snap my fingers and make it disappear," he shook his head, "much as I hate to admit it, she is much more powerful than I am. The magic seems to be sort of self-replicating. I can take some away, like this," he touched me and I felt a momentary respite from the vertigo, but then it was back full force. "See," he said. "It just fills you up again."

"Can you get her, whoever her is, to undo it?"

He laughed. "Right now, she won't even give the time of day. And the lady in question is Hecate. Not exactly a lady, rather a very powerful Goddess."

I stared at him, mouth open. This was just nuts.

"You don't believe me."

"No."

"Why does no one ever believe me?" he asked no one in particular, holding out his hand to help me up.

I stumbled to my feet, swaying slightly and trying to get the insides of my head to come to a stop. "Who are you?" I asked.

Archimedes sucked in his breath.

"It's all right. She has never met me before. I'm Lucifer, the Morning Star."

"You're the Devil? Satan?" This was so far over the top we'd gone completely around and come out the bottom,

"No, the Devil and Satan are different. Actually there are several Satans. I'm Lucifer, the fallen angel. Sent here to Hell" he held up his arms to indicate the room.

"This is Hell?"

He sighed, dramatically. "Yes, my dear, Earth is Hell. God exiled me here to live amongst you humans after I told him how flawed you all are, an unworthy creation. He didn't take constructive criticism well and refused to acknowledge he wasn't the only deity in the universe."

I just shook my head. Which made the vertigo worse. I held out my arms to steady myself and Lucifer reached out to give me his arm. Heat shot into me. Clarity restored itself in my brain and body.

"While you stay with us, I suggest you reflect on your attitude," he said, arching an eyebrow at me.

"What attitude would that be?" He sounded like my mom. I could feel my shoulders tensing.

"The whole 'victim' thing you've got going on." He acted out the quote marks. Bastard.

"Victim?" I wanted to yell at him.

"Now, get those hormones back under control. I know you're only sixteen, but that excuse won't work down here. The poor little me, I killed my brother and broke up my parent's marriage, so I'm going to live my life as a loner."

"But I did," I screamed.

He snapped his fingers and out of nowhere a wave of cold water slapped me in the face. He continued, "I said, 'no attitude'. Yes, you killed your brother in an accident. Forgive yourself, you were a kid. Your parent's marriage was their problem, you just ended up with the fallout, but you weren't the cause. It wasn't strong enough to weather adversity. Now, I'm done with my lecture."

I'm sure my mouth hung wide open. How could he have known about the accident?

Dad had taken me hunting for the first time, with 'the guys'. I felt clumsy and rushed. I don't remember a lot about it. Except that I screwed up the two most basic things about guns, always pay attention to where you're pointing your gun and always leave the safety on.

As they loaded Chris into the helicopter, I'll never forget the look Dad gave me. It was such a look of disgust. It felt like he'd just punched me. He hasn't spoken to me since. So yeah, I felt like a victim, even though I killed Chris. I also felt like I killed my parent's marriage, if I hadn't killed him, they'd probably still be together. I caused the adversity. He was right about one thing though. Two years ago, I'd still been a kid. Killing someone you love makes you grow up fast.

He turned to the dog-headed man and said, "Anubis, would you please find her a room, and procure her some food and cooler clothes to wear. She'll roast down here." He looked at me again. "I'll try to help you, see if I can unravel some of her magic, but we are in the middle of a war. I don't have much time for you."

Anubis bowed and left the room.

I wanted to hit him. Instead I asked, "War. With who?" I looked around. There was nothing around me that spoke of war. I felt confused.

"War. With Hecate of course."

# CHAPTER THREE

OH, of course. I should have known. Hecate. Who was that? What was this all about? I must have just stood there looking stupid, because he spoke again.

"Hecate, Goddess of the Underworld, magic, etc. Ever heard of her?"

"Vaguely."

"You humans," he said with disgust. "She's one of the most powerful deities and you've vaguely heard of her."

I didn't want to point out that the Greek gods and goddesses had pretty much died when the Roman Empire took over. "Why are you at war with her?"

"We've been in a relationship for a couple thousand years and she thinks I cheated on her."

"Did you?" I asked, wondering where I'd gotten the nerve to ask such a question.

"As if. Not that it's any of your business." He stood hands on his hips, reminding me of a petulant teenager. I almost laughed, but thought it might not be the best idea.

Anubis came back, presumably to show me to my room. At the same time a yellow man with huge horns came running in. He carried a shield and wore a handgun strapped to his waist. Lucifer went up to him and they spoke in whispers, then the horned man left.

Lucifer turned to me and said, "Anubis will show you to a room and you can change. I've got to attend to a few things. He will show you around and explain who to stay away from. Not all my creatures do well around humans."

I looked over at mirror man. "What about him?"

"You want to stay away from him. He's definitely not safe and he doesn't owe you anymore." Lucifer stared at me, making me uncomfortable.

I looked away. "Why can't I just go home?"

"Not in this state. You're carrying too much magic which you can't handle right now." He turned away, dismissing me. He clapped his hands and spoke in a language I couldn't understand. The inhabitants of the room stopped whatever they were doing, stood and ran, galloped or flew out the doors; some of them looked very grim. Not that I knew what they normally looked like. The playful feeling of the room had vanished.

I followed Anubis, down a hallway and into a small room. There was a bed, table and chairs, television and bathroom. Other than the fact that there were no windows, it looked like a hotel room. The decor was all in red and gold like everything I'd seen so far. Gaudy.

Anubis said in a rough voice, "There are clothes in the closet for you. I'll be back in half an hour to show you around. Then he left, closing the door.

I sat on the bed and pried my Docs off. I was sweltering, even though my clothes were wet from the shower Lucifer had given me. I peeled off my socks and turned the TV on with a remote. I flipped through all the local channels, lots of cable channels, plus HBO, Showtime and way too many ESPN channels and found something called HellTV. A woman with red wings, hair and eyes sat at a news desk and spoke into the camera.

"Alexa Daniova with the news. It's Friday, July 13, here in Hell and word has just come in Hecate has launched an attack. Many of her animals, dogs, horses and snakes, have overrun Hell, attacking us. A blue mist has been seen swirling around the tunnels. No one seems to know what it is or if it's dangerous. There have been possible fatalities and many injuries from the attack."

At this the screen went blank and the lights in my room went out. It was pitch black in the room and I couldn't see. While trying to find my boots and socks, I bumped into every piece of furniture. I felt tense and scared, my senses on alert. Loud thumping noises sounded in the hall and an eerie screeching rang out. Every now and then I could see light under my door, maybe someone passing with a torch.

I finally found the nerve to creep over to the door. Shoulders tensed and blood pounding in my ears, I turned the doorknob and peered out. In the dim light a massive pig with tusks was running down the hall snorting and chasing one of the dog-headed men. I closed the door and stood against it, trying to lock it. There was no lock. Maybe no one would look for me.

There was a pounding at the door. I silently backed away in the general direction of the bathroom.

Then I tripped over my boot and fell backwards.

The door swung open and luminous blue mist filled the room, lighting it.

A huge man with a sword and shield came in and spotted me instantly.

I sat there, frozen. The dizziness made me feel like retching.

"Now, what have we here?"

A skinny man in animal skins walked in. "A live human. What is he doing with a human? Bring her," he said, sneering.

The first man grabbed my arm and pulled me up.

"My boots," I said. "I need my boots." I was stalling, trying to think of a way out of this. The hallway had turned into a highway filled with people. It didn't look like a good escape route.

"You don't need boots."

"I'll cut my feet." There were no windows. The door was the only way out, these two clearly wouldn't leave me alone.

The second man laughed.

The first man whistled and called out, "Sarah."

A whinny answered and in trotted a delicate, dapple gray mare.

The large man sheathed his sword and hauled me up onto her

back. I felt like a piece of baggage. "Keep your head low," he warned me, then slapped the mare on her rump. She turned and took off out the door.

We raced down the corridor and people flattened themselves against the wall as I clenched her mane tightly, trying not to slip off and get stomped on by the crowd. I thought about trying to escape, but the mare wouldn't pay attention to what I wanted. I'm not a good rider, even with a saddle, and the world was spinning. Once or twice she leapt over something or someone on the floor. We went in and out of pools of darkness until we came to the room where Lucifer had first greeted me. I felt really awful by then.

The blue mist hung so thickly I could hardly see. A tall, thin woman with jet black hair stood by the door. She had a crescent moon tattooed on her forehead and a silver crescent moon around her neck. With her blue-white eyes, she looked at the mare, then me and said, "Go through the portal."

The mare leapt into a patch of darkness I hadn't noticed. My vertigo became so intense that I lost my balance and fell.

# CHAPTER FOUR

I WOKE to bright light shining in my eyes. It was so glaring I could barely see. I felt like I'd drunk too much wine. I tried sitting up but when I moved the dizziness overwhelmed me, so I just lay there, waiting for my eyes to adjust. The scent of honeysuckle or jasmine, I couldn't tell which, filled the air. My brain felt foggy and thinking wasn't compatible with my existence.

"She's waking. Go tell Hecate."

I heard footsteps running away.

I could barely make out the form of a man. I lay on a hard couch in a sunny room. Probably not in Seattle if there was sun. The room was stuffed with plants and had a high ceiling made of windows. Like a huge fancy greenhouse.

When I turned my head, I was eye to eye with a large dog. A dark, brown hound with soulful, yellow eyes. I tried to recall my knowledge from memorizing dog books as a kid, but couldn't figure out what breed exactly. He had that doggy smell which reminded me of Coal, a lab we had when I was a kid. Well, Chris had him. That dog loved Chris best of all, Just like everyone else.

The man grew clearer, shoulder length dark hair and a kind face smiled at me. He wore olive green pants and a rough, leather shirt.

Brown, soft leather boots and a belt from which hung a knife in a sheath. If I was in a movie, I'd peg him for Robin Hood.

There was movement from the other side of the room, a tall woman with long silver hair. She wore sleek black pants and a silver tunic. Large silvery wings folded across her back. I could see a netlike pattern on them and her clothes as well. A chain circled her neck and from it hung a huge teardrop shaped black stone set beside a silver moon. Her light blue eyes were striking as they stared at me. Two small, black snakes curled around her arms. Live snakes.

"Finally awake, I see."

"Where am I?"

"No where that would make any sense to you. Now, tell me who you are and why you were with Lucifer, and I might let you live."

I debated whether to answer her. "I'm Angelica Monroe. I'm not with Lucifer. I was walking around my neighborhood in Seattle, when I found a free mirror. I took it home and found this guy in it. So I broke the mirror to let him out and I got infected by the magic, or so he said. He took me to Lucifer to try to fix me. Then all hell broke loose. And now I'm here."

"Interesting story," she said.

"Who are you?"

"I'm Hecate."

"Please tell me, where am I?"

"Ah, that we will not reveal, other than to say this is my domain. But you are safe and you will not leave here until I say you will. Nuada will see to that," she nodded toward the dog. He bayed in answer to her and the loud sound hurt my ears.

I realized the room had been filling up with animals: dogs, horses and boars. Some sat still, others wove around each other. Snakes slithered up the plants. I saw now that the man in green had a small snake on his shoulders. I looked at it nervously. I hate snakes. We used to have a lot of rattlesnakes out in the vineyards. I shivered just at the sight of them.

Hecate must have noticed because she said, "They will not harm you here. They are my creatures." She put her hand down and another one slithered up her arm, wrapping itself around her shoulder and beneath her hair.

It was good they wouldn't harm me, because I didn't feel like going anywhere. The vertigo was too overwhelming. As I fell back asleep, the musky scent of lilies filled the air.

I don't know how long I slept, but it felt like a day or two. Someone would occasionally thrust food and water at me or escort me to the bathroom but mostly I slept, hearing voices and movement but unable to make any sense of them.

When I did finally wake, it was gray and cloudy above. Nuada sat with his head resting on my couch, staring at me as if he could see everything I thought and felt.

The Robin Hood man came in and asked, "Would you like to get up?"

"Please," I said. I slowly sat up. I found if I didn't make any sudden movements the vertigo didn't completely wipe me out, but it was still noticeable.

A short, red haired woman came in and led me to a pool for bathing. I undressed and cleaned myself up then dressed in the clothes they'd laid out for me. Mine were gone. Black pants and shirt and socks. But they'd brought my Docs. I brushed my tangled hair and was led to another room with a buffet table weighed down with food.

Starving, I nearly inhaled sausage and eggs, scones and hot coffee. No one else was in the room except Nuada and I. I gave him some sausage which he scarfed down.

"You like that, boy?"

He barked in response so I gave him more.

"You have a kind heart," said a voice.

I smelled lilies again, looked up and saw Hecate leaning against the doorway.

"I was taught to share."

"And how are you sharing your gifts with the world?"

"I don't have any gifts," I said. "I'm only good at destruction."

She laughed at me. I gripped my fork tightly and jammed it into the eggs.

"I do not think destruction is one of your gifts. If it was you would have killed yourself by now. Instead, you are still alive although slowly making a mess of your life."

"So what are my gifts?" I was challenging her. "How is it that everyone else knows my life?".

"I think I'll give you a task to complete so you can discover your gifts and see how precious your life is," she said, sliding into a chair at the table and taking a sausage off my plate.

"I don't want any task. All I want is for things to be back the way they were before I killed my brother." I pulled my plate away and sucked down the remaining sausage.

"My dear, even I can't turn back time." She stared at me. I could almost see the wheels turning. I didn't like the way she was looking at me.

"I don't want any task."

"You want to go back to your cozy, sheltered world. But it never really existed. Life isn't like that. Have you forgotten how much you and your brother fought? You were always jealous of him and the fact that your father always favored him and your mother respected him more because he was the up and coming winemaker. And everything you did to help the family business was grudgingly given."

I gripped my cup tightly. Everything she said was true and it pissed me off.

"I still don't have any gifts and I don't want to challenge myself."

"You never have. You've always been afraid of not living up to your brother's more obvious gifts." She got up and went to the buffet table and loaded up a plate. She sat back down across from me.

I sat and sipped my coffee watching her wolf down food. When she finished she leaned the chair back on two legs and belched the hugest belch I've ever heard. I almost laughed.

"Your problem," she said, stretching out her wings which were about six feet long, "is that you are living within the structure of society's confines. I know, I know, you think you're not. You're a loner, always have been. Home schooled, though not the type of homeschooling done by conservative Christians, since your parents are atheists. But you're still stuck following too many of society's rules.

You're only sixteen and still living at home so that's understandable. But you're not going to find out who you are until you break away from those rules."

"What rules?" I asked, wanting to strangle her.

"The ones about being polite to everyone to the point of harming yourself. Not standing up for yourself. Not taking any risks about who you want to be for fear of making the wrong choice. Your brother knew what he wanted to be from the moment he first tasted wine. Your path is different. Unfortunately, you'll need to flounder around and try things, making mistakes until you figure it out. You won't do that by trying to please your mother and there'll be no pleasing your father until he recovers from his son's death and realizes he's lost his daughter."

What she said felt true even though I didn't want to admit it out loud. I needed to make myself happy. "I don't know what to do," I admitted, petting Nuada's soft ears. He sat with his muzzle resting on my knee. When he was touching me the vertigo didn't disable me.

"You should start by admitting that killing your brother was an accident. Every time that voice in your head says you murdered him slap it around and tell it to get out. Then start working on the one that says you were responsible for the failure of your parent's marriage. They may have made you the scapegoat but the reality was it's between the two of them and they're wrong to put any of the blame on you."

"But losing their son made their lives unbearable."

"Grief is a hard thing but if that's all it took to total their marriage it must have been pathetic to start with. You have a chance to make a new start this fall. A new school in a new town where no one knows anything about you. You can be whoever you want to be. You don't have to be sad, loner Angelica who killed her brother, broke up her parent's marriage and who'd rather sit in her room listening to music and curled up with a book than talk to anyone. You could even try making some friends."

"I don't know how," I said.

"You're sixteen. Time to learn. Even though you humans have pitifully short lives, they seem very long if you're alone."

I nodded. And swirled a spoon around in what remained in the bottom of my coffee cup. Nuada moved his head, trying to get it underneath my hand. When I touched him, I felt a calm, confidence descend over me. "Why don't I feel like the room is whirling around when Nuada is touching me?"

"He's a powerful being. He's bleeding off some of the excess magic that you don't know yet how to control." She rocked on the back legs of her chair again, feet bracing on the trestle underneath the table.

Something she said stuck in my brain. "What do you mean, that I don't know yet how to control? Lucifer said he was going to remove it. I was assuming you could do the same."

"No. You've been under its influence too long. I'm not even sure I could have removed it when you first were infected. It burrowed into that black hole you're carrying around in your chest. I couldn't remove it without destroying you." She stared at me intently. Her light blue eyes burned right through me.

"So, I'm going to feel dizzy for the rest of my life?"

"There is an alternative."

"What?" I asked.

"You could learn to use the magic. That would take care of your dizziness."

My mouth was hanging open. "I don't even believe in magic let alone believe I can learn how to use it."

"Oh, well then let's just forget it," she said, moving to rise. "You can spend the rest of your life attached to a magical creature but you better hope he doesn't disappear because then you'll be stuck with vertigo. And there won't be anyone around to help you. I've got a lot to do and I won't be hanging around watching you make a mess of your life."

I'd gone too far and felt ashamed of myself. Why was I always so rude? "I'm sorry," I said. "I didn't mean to offend you. It's just hard to believe that I can do magic. I've hardly ever seen it."

"Open your eyes, dear girl. What do you think that mirror was? And the portal that brought you here? And I'm certain most of what you saw with Lucifer was magic. He's fabulous at smoke and mirrors. He's even fooled me on occasion."

She stood and turned her back to me while she poured coffee. Her wings looked constricted and her body rigid. It made me wonder exactly what happened between the two of them for a war to break out.

The Robin Hood guy came in the room and cleared his throat. Hecate looked at him and he came towards her. There was a whispered conversation. Her eyes narrowed and the coffee cup she held clenched in her hand shattered and fell to the floor. She shook her hand as if to dry it. The coffee, hung in midair as if gravity didn't exist, then fell with a splat joining the pieces of the mug.

"Bloody hell," she said and stormed out of the room, creating a small whirlwind as she went, blowing the tablecloth, napkins and detaching leaves from the plants.

He turned to me, bowed and said, "I am Eren. If you are finished with breakfast, Nuada will take you to the solarium, where you will be safest."

"Safest, what's going on?"

"We are under attack. Nuada, go now." He ran out of the room, following Hecate.

Nuada stood and barked at me. I grabbed a couple of croissants and a pear, not knowing when I'd be able to eat again. I followed Nuada back to the glass room with all the plants. Somehow a glass room didn't seem all that safe to me. Not during a war. But I didn't know what weapons they were using to fight. What weapons did gods use against each other? Except Lucifer wasn't a god, but a fallen angel. So did that make him more or less powerful than Hecate?

# CHAPTER FIVE

NUADA and I curled up on the couch. I buried my face in his soft fur, smelling that lovely doggy smell and trying to pretend I was a world away. We were surrounded by the baying of hounds, roaring and a whole lot of banging. His ears twitched at the sounds, following the battle. At one point, the door opened and the tall, thin woman who let me through the portal at Lucifer's looked in. She must have been satisfied that we were safe because she left and closed the door. The door glowed with golden light and I could smell smoke in the air which wafted through. Nuada put his head in my lap and napped a little. I nibbled on my croissants, wishing I'd brought some coffee with me.

I thought about the conversation Hecate and I had. Was it possible to change who I was as much as she said? I thought I'd have to carry Chris' death with me forever. It was a heavy chain, dragging me down to the bottom of the river. Could I actually cut the chain and swim to shore? Become someone new?

What would a me look like who could use magic? Would I live in the real world? Or would I have to live in this bizarre place or Lucifer's even stranger place? Or were they the same? The more I thought, the more questions I found.

The door flung open. Nuada jumped up and stood staring, head down and ready to attack. My whole body tensed, not knowing what to do.

A red glow preceded Lucifer into the room. He wore a sheepish smile on his face. Then I noticed a snake wrapped around his neck like a leash. Hecate held the other end. She looked grim. Following her was a pack of dogs made up of several different breeds, all of which looked fierce. Nuada seemed unfazed by them, keeping his eyes on Lucifer.

"I came to get you back," he said. "I gave my word that I'd try to help release you from the magic." He shrugged. "But as you can see, my Lady has me under her spell again."

"And my quandary is what to do with you now. I should torture you," said Hecate.

"You know I love a good torture," he said.

"Yes, that's what worries me. Perhaps something else. A true punishment." Hecate looked royally pissed off. I felt glad it wasn't aimed at me.

Nuada sat down beside me, keeping an eye on Lucifer, as if he wasn't to be trusted. Every now and then he let out a throaty growl.

Hecate said, "You couldn't have released her from the magic anyway. It's gone too deep."

Lucifer looked at me intently. "Aah. I can see that now. But I did so want to be a hero."

Hecate snapped the snake at him. "Being a hero doesn't become you. At least not one who lies to look good."

He said to me, "She's so far above me with magic. It's like comparing a raindrop to the ocean. She is after all a child of the Titans, created long before I was even thought of."

I watched the two of them wrangle, trying to figure out their twisted relationship, but it was way beyond me. I'd never met anyone remotely like the two of them. I just wanted to leave, but since Hecate seemed to be in battle mode, it didn't seem like a good time to ask.

Eventually, she seemed bored and called out, "Selene." The tall, dark haired woman came and Hecate handed her Lucifer's snake leash. "Take him to the green room and lock the door."

Selene nodded and led Lucifer away. He looked dejected.

"What will you do with him?" I asked.

"A few days in the green room will lower the cockiness level a bit," she said. The dogs relaxed as Lucifer left. They lay down at her feet.

"What's in the green room?"

"You don't want to know. He'll live. He is immortal remember."

"Do you torture all your lovers?"

She glared at me.

"You told me to stop being polite." It was the only defense I could come up with for being so nosy.

She laughed so hard, she started to cry. I wasn't prepared for that. Nuada looked nervous.

"That was really good," she said. "Not that it's any of your business, but I haven't had any other lovers since him. That's a couple thousand years of monogamy. And he actually enjoys being chastised."

I felt stunned. Here was this goddess, over 2,000 years old, I couldn't remember when the Greeks lived, who'd only had one lover in that long a time. She was gorgeous. Were the other gods that afraid of powerful women? Okay, stupid question. My passing familiarity with mythology told me yes. Zeus was married, but screwed any human woman who took his fancy while his wife sat home twiddling her thumbs. Hades tricked Persephone to trap her into staying with him. And the Christian God, I wasn't even going to think about that. Although since so many people (men) had their hands in writing the bible, there's no clarity there about what God may actually have thought or said. It'd had all been filtered through whatever culture the writers lived in. I don't think any of those cultures had much respect for women as thinking, equal beings. So, looking at it that way Hecate really didn't have much to choose from.

"Excuse me for saying this, Lucifer was the best you could do?"

"What do you think is wrong with Lucifer?" Hecate looked at me, arms crossed. She was scrutinizing me.

"Didn't you accuse him of cheating on you?"

"Yes, I did. It was a test. He passed."

"How was it a test?" Were relationships of immortal beings that different from humans? This made no sense to me.

"I knew he hadn't cheated on me. Most beings are transparent to me. And Lucifer, while less powerful than I, is still very powerful and wonderfully gifted. It was a test to see what he'd do with the accusation."

"And what did he do?" I asked

"He was hurt. I stormed and yelled at him. He calmly told me I was wrong and retreated to his lair to sulk. When I attacked he defended his domain, but no more. Finally, after I refused to speak with him, he attacked here. Although he surrendered too easily, I thought."

"But what about all the people who were killed?"

"What people who were killed?" she asked, amused.

"When I was there I watched something called HellTV. It talked about deaths and casualties."

"Aah. That is Lucifer's propaganda. His way of saving face. No one was killed, I would have known if my creatures or people killed anyone. You see, if Lucifer could claim there were deaths to his people, he'd have a reason to attack me, thus giving himself a way to surrender gracefully, because I will always be much more powerful."

"None of this makes any sense." My head was beginning to hurt. Way too much thinking about things way beyond me.

"I suppose it wouldn't to a young human. It's all tactical. Lucifer and I have lived in the world for a very long time."

"Why does no one know you are alive?"

"Many beings know I'm alive," Hecate said, amused.

"I mean humans."

"There are still humans who believe in me. But it's of no benefit to show myself. I rarely need the help of humans and I don't need to be worshipped or troubled by their problems."

"Is the same true of God?"

"Now which god are we speaking of?" she asked, smiling.

"You know, the Christian God with the capital G."

"Ah him. Well, he's mellowing with age, he's been vastly misunderstood and he knows it. It pains him what humans have done with his words, so he speaks rarely and only to a few who can keep his words silent. I don't think he needs worship either. He'd prefer humans simply loved each other and treated each other kindly."

Safe answer, I thought.

"Well, I must really be going. I've got a battle to mop up and my creatures to see to. Have Nuada take you for a walk. Tomorrow, we'll discuss what you've decided to do." Hecate swirled out of the room, followed by the pack of dogs.

# CHAPTER SIX

NUADA and I walked through the halls. There lay clumps of fur, dropped weapons, and occasionally a downed creature being tended by someone. It was hard to categorize things in this world. Was it a man or a creature if he had a human body with a bull's head? What if she had a human head, angel's wings and a cat's body with human hands? I didn't even have names for these beings, although I recognized a sphinx and a chimera.

"Nuada, is there somewhere outside you can take me?" It felt stuffy in the hallways.

Nuada led me to a doorway which opened out on a large veranda. It was dusk, but I could see we were high up on a cliff, the sound of the ocean pounding far below. Mountains lay silhouetted in the distance. I couldn't see what was behind me because of the height of the building. A crescent moon hung on the horizon, just rising or setting. It was an orangish color as if there were smoke or debris in the air.

I wondered what time it was back in Seattle and whether Mom was home yet. I'd written the note about not waiting up. Was this like the magic in books and movies where time stopped in the normal world or had it been days and she was calling the cops? Would she even notice my absence between her endless phone calls and meetings?

Nuada nudged my leg. He looked up at me with his big yellow eyes.

"I know, that's not fair. She's just trying to make a life for us. I just wish it included some time with me."

Nuada slurped at my hand with his tongue. The breeze felt cool and cleansing, and smelled wonderful. Where were we? Where had the gods hid themselves from humans? It wasn't warm here, like I pictured Greece, so I guessed we were somewhere else.

What choices would I have to make tomorrow? To do magic or be stuck with a magical being glued to me or disabled? To change who I was or continue to be loner/loser Angelica? I didn't feel up to making any choices. I couldn't picture anything except what I'd been for the last two years.

Who did I want to be?

# CHAPTER SEVEN

THE NEXT MORNING Nuada woke me by barking. At least he thought it was morning. I'd slept, but the glass ceiling told me it was still night. The candles around the room were lit. I rolled over and tried to go back to sleep, but he pulled off my blanket and kept barking.

"Okay, I'm up. I'm up." I felt refreshed, but why was it so dark? I pulled on a new set of clothes, black again and laced up my docs.

Nuada sat by the door, waiting.

I followed him down the hall to the breakfast room. It was a grand room with two long tables surrounded by chairs, filled with more strange beings. Against two walls stood a buffet table weighed down with food.

A huge boar passed by us on the way into the room. Bowls of all sorts lined up on the floor, against the walls. Most were empty.

I recognized Eren. Also Lucifer's dog-headed man, Anubis. And Archimedes who looked at me hungrily. The more time I spent around him the creepier he got. Nuada growled at him and Archimedes immediately became fascinated by his plate.

I grabbed an empty plate from the buffet table and filled it up with sausage, biscuits and gravy, while wondering if one of the boars had provided the sausage. I put a steak on my plate for Nuada and got myself a cup of coffee as well.

The dark haired woman entered. She saw me and said, "We haven't been introduced. I'm Selene."

"Angelica," I said. I made a move to shake hands, but realized my hands were full. She nodded and got a cup of coffee. She wore a charm bracelet made of crescent moons. With the moon tattoo on her forehead, I wondered if she was a Moon Goddess.

There was an empty chair next to Eren, so I took it. I felt famished, so I dove into eating, as did Nuada, while the conversation rolled on.

"Yes," said Eren. "I believe she visited him last night. It'll be better for all of us if they mend this rift. However, I'm not sure if he's still in the green room or not."

"I hope this ends. Two hundred years is a long time to be at war," said Anubis.

"I miss Endymion," said Selene, sitting down. "I haven't dared contact him since all this began. I know he's still back at Lucifer's Lair."

"Well, we'll find out in the next few days," said Eren. "I hope he has the good sense to apologize."

"Apologize for what?" asked Archimedes. "You don't really think there was infidelity involved?"

"I only know what Hecate says. I'm guessing she won't be happy without a major apology. If he wants her trust, that's what he'll do," said Eren.

"Well, then that's what he'll do," said Anubis. "He knows which side his bread is buttered on."

The conversation ceased abruptly as Hecate entered the room, preceded by five dogs who snarled at each other while claiming various bowls. She took a plate and piled it high with food.

"Did you change your hair?" asked Selene, staring at Eren.

"I'm growing it a little longer," said Eren.

"Trying to attract one of those naiads?" she teased.

Eren sighed. "I know it's hopeless, but I can't seem to stop trying."

Anubis laughed.

Archimedes finished eating, got up and left. His empty plate, cup and utensils vanished. I was astonished watching him do that, but tried hard to keep my mouth shut. Anubis bowed to Hecate and left.

Selene sipped her coffee delicately and stared at me. The silence at the table felt uncomfortable, I squirmed in my chair although not enough to break contact with Nuada. That touching had become second nature and I only stopped, for more than a minute or two, when I wanted to test if the vertigo might have gone away on its own. So far it hadn't. And I also liked touching him. He made me feel safe and life hadn't felt safe for a very long time. I hadn't realized how much I missed that feeling.

Hecate was humming and twisting something with her fingers. Something silver I saw. She was forming it, shaping it into a heart with a small loop on top. Then she blew on it. It glowed like something alive. She pulled off a thin crimson ribbon which had been woven into her silver shirt. Threading the ribbon through the loop, she tied it. Then she handed it to Eren, "Keep this next to your heart for three days, then give it to the naiad. It will work if she has any feelings for you."

He stood and bowed, "Thank you my Lady." He put the heart around his neck, inside his shirt and smiling, left the room.

Hecate turned to me. And stared. I tried to ignore her, but those eyes were impossible to ignore.

Finally, I turned to her and asked, "What?"

"You know what. What have you decided?"

"I have questions," I said, putting down my fork.

She raised her eyebrows.

I continued, "If I choose to learn magic, will I have to stay here, wherever here is, or can I go back to Seattle?"

"Once you learn what you need, you may return home."

Somehow, there seemed to be a trick there. "So how long will it take me to learn?"

"That depends on how hard you work. It may take a month or years."

That felt discouraging.I leaned back in my chair, drooping a little. "So, if I choose a magical animal instead of learning how to use magic, then I could leave now?" I wanted to stay with Nuada. I rubbed my hand down his head and neck, then petted the velvety drooping ears.

"Yes." She drank her coffee and exchanged looks with Selene. I had no idea what passed between them.

"Would the animal be Nuada?" I stared at the hound, whose head rested on my lap.

"Ah, you've fallen in love with Nuada. He does have that effect. I would have to think about that. He is one of my favorites. Although you humans live pathetically short years he would return to me fairly quickly. I will think about it if you make that choice. A snake would be easier to conceal though. If I understand your world correctly, there are places dogs are not welcome."

"I could claim he was a service dog and that he was working. He'd have to wear a vest, but he could go where ever I went then."

"Well, Nuada does like to dress up."

Nuada barked.

"Any more questions?" The eyebrow raised again.

Hecate was really annoying me. It was as if she already knew which direction I'd go. I hated being predictable. But I wouldn't change my mind just to be obstinate. "I choose to learn magic, although I really don't want to lose the chance to be with Nuada."

"Ah, you want things both ways. Humans always were a greedy lot," she laughed and sat back in her chair, spreading her wings to get them out of the way. She gestured to Selene. "Selene will be your teacher. She is a Moon Goddess, one of the Titans as well. She is like a sister to me."

Selene nodded at me. "When you finish eating we will get started."

I nodded back and felt nervous. Would I be able to learn this?

# CHAPTER EIGHT

I STOOD on the veranda and tried once again to feel the magic pulsing out of my body and then to shape it into a shield. I'd done it once before, just barely, but hadn't been able to sustain it or do it again.

Selene sighed with disappointment. She stood silent for a little longer, while I struggled. Then after while she said, "Nuada, show her how to do it."

Nuada, who lay at my feet, stood and pressed his head against my thigh. I relaxed and could feel him drawing energy from the earth below us. He pushed it through our bodies and suddenly we had a glowing, gold aura surrounding us. I felt a rush of energy flow through me, filling me up. I wanted to wallow in it.

Selene said, "Remember how that feels. Let it sink into every pore of your body. Soak it up."

And I did.

Then I could recreate it every time. It turned out Nuada was my best teacher.

After that my learning sped up. I could take the earth's energy and let it mingle with the magic which infected me. Then I learned how to do things with it. I couldn't seem to use my magic all by itself, but I was able to shift energy in a room and transform an item into something else. It was like quantum physics, moving particles around and recombining them into different things. Amazing.

The catch was that no matter how fast my learning went, I still couldn't bleed off enough of the magic to keep myself from being dizzy. I still needed Nuada around constantly. He didn't seem to mind, but I did. Even though I was reevaluating my life and trying to be open with being someone other than Angelica the loner, I wasn't there yet. I was still most comfortable alone. And I hadn't been alone since the day I took that mirror home.

One day I asked Hecate about it. She was on the veranda perched on the stone fence in a very Un-goddess-like pose. At her feet lay six hounds and a boar, stretched out sleeping.

"Why do I still have so much magic inside me; I can't use it up fast enough."

"You absorbed a great deal of magic. It took a large amount to put him in the mirror. He stayed there for centuries and the magic built up, siphoning off his. You got hit with almost all of it. The magic you have done so far is quite low energy magic. You may need to work your way up to something as large as sustaining the borders of a land like this."

My eyes widened. "Is that what you do?"

"That's one of the things I do. Not consciously, mind you. I just set it up and the protective borders spin out on their own, drawing energy from me."

"What do you need protection from?" It worried me that a goddess with her power would need protection.

"There are many powerful beings out there, some who would harm my people." She rubbed one of her hound's back with a foot. "Many of them would love to neutralize me."

I shivered. "Who are they?"

"Best you not know."

"Do they have a chance to harm you?"

She looked at me strangely. "Of course they do. I'm strong, but not invincible. But I cannot be killed, I am a Titan and a goddess of the Underworld."

"You say, 'a goddess' as if there's more than one for the Underworld."

"You really do need to brush up on your mythology, my dear. Nearly every culture has a god or goddess or both, of the Underworld. Some cultures have multiple deities for the Underworld. Since I am one of the Titans, my domain extends far beyond the Underworld."

"So are we in the Underworld now?" I felt confused about how everything fit together.

"No. We are in a place that is neither your world or the Underworld."

"What happened to all those gods and goddesses whose cultures died?"

"There are many answers to that. Many are still around. Some of them are stuck in time and some, like Selene and I, continue to watch your people, trying to help where we can, so you don't destroy the planet. Some of the weaker deities have died or transformed. Some have gone to sleep with no intent of awakening. Some chose to become human and live a human life, then died. Some have fought each other and been killed. Some have been turned to stone or otherwise immobilized for attacking others. We are all different and have taken individual paths." She rubbed Nuada's head and he licked her hand.

"I still don't feel any closer to dealing with the excess magic."

"You need a more powerful outlet for it. Be patient. It will come. Still, I think I'll ask Selene to move up your battle training. Things are coalescing in our world. You'll need to defend yourself." She sighed. "I suppose I must heal the rift with Lucifer so that once again we can be unified. We'll be stronger that way. Romantic relationships complicate things so much."

I shrugged. I'd never had one. And none of my friends had, since I didn't have any friends. Mom's life seemed just as complicated now as it was when she was still married to Dad.

Nuada rubbed his head against my thigh. I stroked his ears.

Hecate stood. "Well, I better get this over with." She walked away followed by her furry entourage.

I realized she considered all the animals 'her people' as well as the humans and gods and goddesses under her protection. She treated the animals as sentient. I felt sure Nuada was.

I wondered what would happen between her and Lucifer. It seemed as if all this was a game to her. Was it a game to him as well? Maybe that's what relationships became after thousands of years.

I practiced the shield work some more, wanting to be ready when the storm arrived. I wondered who was strong enough to mount an attack on both Hecate and Lucifer.

# CHAPTER NINE

THE NEXT MORNING Lucifer joined Hecate at breakfast as if they'd never fought. Everyone was smiling. Well, everyone except Archimedes. I'd never seen him smile, other than creepily. I didn't want to know what it would take to get him to smile either. He struck me as stalker/serial killer material.

When I sat down, Lucifer said, "Well, if it isn't our human friend. How are you getting on here?"

"Good," I said, cautiously. I still didn't know whether to trust him or not. He might be a nice guy with a bad rap, or not.

I filled up my plate and grabbed a coffee. Then got another plate for Nuada with the best I could tell was dog appropriate food and set it at my feet.

Hecate said, "Selene will meet you at the armory. Today you start battle training and she can help you find what you do best. It should give you a better outlet for all that magic."

I nodded since my mouth was full. It was then I noticed that everyone else seemed huddled around a screen. Anubis was typing things in and bringing up information.

Finally he said, "That's what we know so far."

Lucifer said to Hecate, "So your intuition was right as usual." He asked Anubis, "How long have we got?"

"Three, maybe four days."

"I need to alert my people and bring them here. We can use the warriors and the rest will be safer here."

"Good," Hecate said. "Erin, step up our plans."

"Yes, my Lady." He ran from the room so fast I hardly saw him move. He was just gone.

Hecate looked at me and said, "You better learn fast or you'll be hiding with the children and at the mercy of anyone who finds you. And the gods are merciless."

I gulped down the rest of my coffee. "Who's attacking us?"

"Hades, Pluto and Arawn. Probably with Zeus behind them," said Hecate.

"Yikes." I stuffed cinnamon roll into my mouth.

"Yikes doesn't begin to cover it," said Lucifer, grimly.

I grabbed the rest of my food and Nuada and I ran from the room. I hung onto his tail as he led me towards the armory I presumed.

Lucifer called down the hallway, "Nuada, be a good boy and take care of her. There might be a reward for you in it." He laughed and I heard a loud smack. "Ouch," he said. "I was just joking."

I didn't know what that whole exchange was about. Best to ignore it. We ran down two flights of stairs and then outside. Across the courtyard was a one story building. Inside I found Selene examining weapons.

"Good, you're early," she said. "Let's get started before this place is packed. Everyone will be here getting weapons and sparring. She grabbed a knife still in its sheath, a bow and arrow and a couple of swords and walked out a back door. A woman called Anya who had webbed hands, and possibly feet, followed us to 'hold the space' and keep my vertigo from overcoming me, so I could spar.

"We're going to use real weapons? On gods and goddesses? Who can't die?" I felt my stomach tie itself into a billion knots.

"Not all of them are immortal and even those who are can be injured. And most of the warriors they'll bring are dead."

"But if they're already dead, what good are these?" I could hear the panic in my voice. I was almost shrieking.

"You are carrying an enormous amount of Hecate's magic. The dead can be killed permanently. They will be unable to reincarnate, gone, kaput. The immortal deities can be brought down so they can't harm anyone for a time. The weaker deities can also be killed, although I'm not sure if you'll be able to summon enough power to do that. You of course can be killed and that will be obvious to all of them."

I nodded at her.

She continued, "These weapons are merely the vehicle. The channel which will carry that magic, along with your intent, to anyone you wish to bring down. You don't have to hit someone hard, just touching them will be enough. The intent, plus your aim is what's important."

"Okay," I said. I still felt dubious this was within my power.

She showed me how to pull the arrow. At first I could only make it fly two feet, before it fell to the ground. It wasn't till the end of the day that I could make it go much further. I got a painful blister from the bow and arrow. We stopped periodically for sword practice. I was glad the edges were blunted and that it really didn't weigh much because after a few minutes it felt like eighty pounds of free weights at the end of one arm. But the point was to send magic through it and by the end of the day I could feel a trickle of it passing through my sword arm and out the end of my sword.

"All you have to do is touch something that's touching someone else. Their sword, armor, skin, their horse. Whatever. Push that intent through to them."

By the end of the day I was toast. My arms and legs felt all rubbery and I could hardly move to walk. Maybe it hadn't even been a whole day. I tended to lose track of time here. Nuada stuck closely to me. I fell asleep at the table.

The next two days were much the same, except that I improved. I could shoot farther, hit a little harder and extend the magic more strongly. Selene made me wear a belt with the knife on it all the time. She said I might actually be able to move my magic past the sword or the arrow if I continued practicing.

Halfway through the fourth day, Hecate came to us and said, "I need Nuada. Now. Angelica you will have to cope without him for the time being. Selene, follow me, Angelica follow Anya to the bunkers, but take your weapons."

I nodded. I hadn't realized before but the dizziness hadn't been around for a day or so.

Anya said, "I will stay with her, if she needs help."

Hecate hadn't waited for an answer. Nuada started to follow her, ran back to me and licked my hand, then ran after Hecate.

Anya led me back to the main building. We went down four flights of stairs, each one narrower than the one before. The staircase had been carved into solid rock.

We went inside a room filled with children and a few adults, some of whom looked ancient. Did gods age? There were some of the more helpless animals here as well. And baby animals. Lots of puppies. Anya had told me there were four bunkers in all.

At some point the door was sealed with golden glowing magic from one of the older women.

The battle began.

# CHAPTER TEN

EXPLOSIONS FILLED the air and the earth around us moved. Dust and small debris fell from the ceiling raining down on us. At times the air became so filled with dust it felt hard to breathe.

Some of the adults tried to entertain the children. Others sat with their heads in their hands. I wondered if the children were dead and if they were newly dead or if they were older than some of the adults.

Puppies and small animals romped around my feet. The smell of the oil lamps felt comforting. A few people had enough magic to make light in other ways. I wished there was a TV with HellTV up and running. Although maybe I didn't really want to know what was happening up there.

I sat on one of the benches, Anya crowded next to me. I couldn't put down the sword; the bow I held between my legs with the case of arrows over my left shoulder. The sword was point down on the stone floor and I grasped it as if my life depended on it.

Above us was a loud explosion and more powdered rock filtered down through the light, looking like mist. I wondered if there was anything left standing above us. Were there any stairs left? Would anyone be able to dig us out or would we starve or die of thirst buried here in the ground? Or die of asphyxiation? Did the dead people among us even need air?

Anya touched my arm and pointed. I was gripping the sword so tightly, it started to glow. I'm not sure what would have happened had I touched anyone with it. I'd channeled so much fear into it though, surely someone would have died of fright. I did the breathing and calming exercises that Selene taught me and the sword lost its golden color. I'd have to ask her about the glowing when I saw her again.

At some point I dozed off. I woke when someone passed food and drink around. I sipped some water and chewed on dried meat and fruit. Very different from the sumptuous table of Hecate. I dozed again, Anya and I leaned our heads together for support.

When I woke things were quiet above. Something must have happened. Someone must have won, but who?

There was thumping and banging outside the door. The stairway must be getting cleared. Those of us with weapons moved towards the door. An elderly man held my sword, while I readied an arrow, sending magic through it. Our lights had been put out. We waited, barely breathing, afraid of who might be out there.

Finally the door was flung open and bright light shone in. A winged figure, dressed all in black stood in the doorway.

He laughed and said, "I'm baaaack." It was Lucifer. I almost wanted to throw a rock at him for the lame Jack Nicholson imitation, but I felt so relieved it was him.

We relaxed and lowered our weapons. Gradually, everyone funneled their way out of the bunker and into the fresh air. The stairway was littered with chunks of the huge stones which had been used to build the walls. As we climbed out, I realized that unlike before when we were four stories underground, now we were two. The entire building and two floors of basement had been destroyed. I felt fearful to find out how many lives had been lost.

The amount of debris was astonishing. We moved toward a field which had been growing vegetables. Now it was entirely trampled and bodies lay about. They were being gathered into two different heaps, which I assumed were *us* and *them*. The *us* pile was interspersed with wood and straw and some sort of dust being sprinkled on as well as a liquid, maybe oil, poured in between layers of carefully laid bodies.

The *them* pile was made of bodies dumped haphazardly in the same area.

Hecate stood in the middle of the field, her clothes, torn, and in some places burned, hair tangled and eyes blazing with anger as she watched the corpses being gathered up. Her two ever-present snakes wound around her upper arms. She was surrounded by tired looking hounds and two boars.

When everyone was present, she said, "We have survived this round. The enemy has retreated. Once we regroup, we will go into hiding. All of us will go to the same place so you can be protected. I have lost many of my children in this battle, but we will prevail."

After that she walked over and stood by the *us* heap of remains. A woman in black robes stood where Hecate had been and began chanting in a language I didn't know. It sounded deep and mournful, tears filled my eyes and sadness consumed my whole body.

Eventually, the corpse collecting seemed to be at an end and those who had been doing that task stood silently around the heap of carcasses. Hecate cried out something I couldn't understand, perhaps it was in Greek, but it became almost an echo to the woman chanting. Then she pointed at the bodies and fire shot out from her hand.

Everyone stepped back as the oil lit and soon the mountain was consumed by flame. People cried and moaned and screamed with grief. I realized that many of the dead must have lived for thousands of years. I hadn't seen anyone I recognized, but I'd only seen a fraction of the beings who lived with Hecate and Lucifer. I cried anyway. What a waste.

I'd been looking and hadn't seen Nuada anywhere. I wondered if Hecate had sent him on an errand somewhere. I hoped he was safe.

The sun was slinking towards the horizon, and the sky shot through with red and orange and hot pink, echoing the fire. It seemed as if the sky was telling the dead goodbye.

From the conversations in the crowd, I got the feeling this was a rushed funeral. Everyone was afraid the enemy would come back and catch us unawares.

I don't know how long the pyre burned. When there was only

smoke and coals left, some of the folks in charge began herding everyone back into the rubble.

I followed, feeling lost and sad. The mass funeral reminded me of Chris and my grief for him came out. I hadn't let all of it out before. How could I since I'd believed for so long that I'd murdered him? Keeping my grief inside was part of my punishment.

I sobbed as I walked along, wondering if any life, short or long was worth anything. I certainly hadn't made much of my short life. I know people say death helps us to appreciate the sanctity of life. For me it only underscored the pathetic futility of it.

When I reached a pair of pillars I noticed Selene standing next to them. A blue and red haze shifted between the pillars. It looked like the portal which had brought me here. When I got closer Selene nodded to me. The flaming sky with all the light made her look torn, tired and dirty.

I stepped through the portal, feeling my body twist inside itself and walked into darkness.

# CHAPTER ELEVEN

WHEN I GOT through and my body twisted back the other way I felt momentarily dizzy and grabbed for the wall to steady myself. But I didn't pass out this time. I just felt like I'd puke.

My eyes adjusted to the dim light and I found myself surrounded by red and gold walls. As we shuffled down a long hallway, I decided we must be at Lucifer's place. There were probably three or four hundred of us refugees. Although some of them might normally live with Lucifer. I was near the end of the line. Air whooshed out as the portal closed and gradually the mass of us moved forward. All of a sudden, I felt crushed by the crowd of dead people. It felt hard to breathe and I started trying to push my way to the side of the hallway, panicking.

I caught sight of a man with long brown hair and golden eyes standing at the side, guiding people along. He looked me in the eyes and sanity returned to me. I could breathe again and the fear sank back down into the pit it came from. He wore green and brown clothes like Eren. I couldn't stop looking at him. He looked about twenty, but was probably some god who was thousands of years old. I sighed and moved on. His gaze filled me up somehow. Made me lose some of the pain and fear of the last few hours. Relief and a feeling of safety and hope spread through me.

At the front of the line a talking boar gave me a floor and room number. A large, blue parrot pointed with his claw in the general direction of where to find it. I went down six floors and towards the end of a corridor was my room. I had some strange neighbors, a woman with an eagle's head and a pair of bears, but then this was Hell.

I opened my door and walked in, switching on the lights. Torches lit up. I turned on HellTV. There was a loop playing which discussed meal times for each floor and showed maps of the place. In an hour there would be an announcement about what exactly happened during the battle. After that would be directions on how to sign up and be assessed for a work position. Everyone was expected to do something, from taking care of the young, to cooking and laundry to battle planning, depending on their skills.

I slipped out of the smoky clothes I'd been wearing for a couple days now and into the shower. The hot water felt lovely. I stood in the shower and cried about feeling lost. Then I washed with the red soap that was provided and used Devil May Care Shampoo followed by Hot Stuff Conditioner. I ended with Satan's Sexy Shimmery Skin Moisturizer. That guy certainly was full of himself, even though he'd said Satan and the Devil were completely different people from him. At least he had a sense of humor.

There were tons of clean clothes in the closet and after rifling through them I finally found some that fit, even if they were gold and gaudy. I took one of my dirty socks, got it wet and used it to shine up my Docs. I ran a brush through my hair and tied it back into a pony tail. Then bagged up all my dirty clothes and put them outside the door as instructed.

The TV showed battle footage. I wondered who shot it. It looked less frightening than it would have in person I felt sure. They had several camera angles. I thought I recognized Zeus. He was throwing massive thunderbolts, bringing sections of Hecate's Palace down and forcing our side into the open. Hades was all in black. He wasn't attacking directly--just sending in horribly grotesque creatures to do his work. The commentary pointed out Arawn, a Celtic God of the Underworld with his pack of hounds and his men fighting in the midst of things. Pluto was seen piling dead bodies onto a cart pulled by four black horses and removing them from the battlefield.

The destruction looked terrible. Even though it was distancing to watch this like a documentary, these were real living, or dead, beings. They'd been vibrant and seemingly alive moments before. Again, I wondered what the point of all this was. Hecate never said what the war was about, simply that we were under attack. I wondered if anything could justify this kind of slaughter. To me all this killing was absolutely wrong. I may have judged myself harshly, but I held others to the same standard.

With all the chaos, I didn't know when I'd get a chance to see Hecate again. To ask about this war. Maybe I did want to leave. Now. But I needed to find out about Nuada. I hadn't seen anyone take prisoners, so I didn't think that could have happened to him. Maybe I could ask Selene, if I saw her.

Although given the staggered mealtimes I wasn't sure if I'd see anyone I knew.

I sat down at the laptop on the small desk. I flipped it open and the home page read: Everything you always wanted to know about Hell, but were afraid to ask. I skimmed through most of it, but got caught up reading: Now That You're Dead....

*You may feel confused about what being dead means. You feel much the same as when you were alive, so we've put together this handy guide to clarify things.*

*Humans: If you're dead you still need to eat, just not as much. The same goes for sleeping. You can be maimed and injured. You can also be permanently killed at which time there's no reincarnation, just nothingness, it's the end of the line. Oh, and for everyone's sake, please bathe.*

*After a time here you will probably choose to reincarnate and return to the human world. Or you can decide that Hell is so much fun you'd just like to stay.*

*In Hell you will learn to take responsibility for yourself and practice things you weren't able to accomplish in life. This will prepare you to reincarnate and to make Hell better for everyone. Here in the Underworld you will encounter many beings you didn't on earth. Since* you can be killed permanently it would be smart to think before you open your mouth.

*Deities and Magical Creatures:* Although you probably aren't dead if you're reading this, most of you can still be killed, some can't. You know who you are. Those who die are gone for good. No reincarnation, no second chances, so live your life here well. You don't need to eat, but trust us, the food down here is so fabulous you won't be able to help yourself. You don't need to sleep. You can all be injured, even permanently by those more powerful than you. Which means you need to behave yourselves and be kind to each other. It's difficult with so many of us, from so many different cultures and some of us have massive egos, but we're asking everyone to make an effort. Being careful of the humans around us is a given if you want to stay here. Remember they've lived much shorter lives than most of you, so have less life experience to draw upon.

Those of you with tremendous amounts of power to burn should consider going to the Healers' to help out.

A chime rang and a female voice which reminded me of a phone operator said, "Now is the mealtime for your floor. Please proceed to dining room B. Thank you."

I strapped on my knife, since I was told never to be without it and stashed the sword, bow and arrows underneath the bed.

Then I went out the door and followed the crowd down the hallway.

As I entered the dining room, an overpowering fragrance of bacon hit me nose. Eren came up to me and said, "Angelica, how are you doing?"

"Okay, I guess. A little disoriented, but okay. Better than you, it looks like." He had a red slice across his eyebrow, with a bruised lump growing beneath it.

"Oh, it looks worse than it feels. It'll be gone tomorrow. How is your vertigo?" He asked, leading me to a table filled with platters of food. The smells made my mouth water. I wondered how long it had been since I ate a proper meal.

"It's still gone, but I miss Nuada terribly. Have you seen him? Is he all right?"

"I haven't seen him since after the battle, but he'll be working right now."

"Working?" I scrunched up my face in confusion.

"Yes, didn't you know? He's a healer."

"Oh." I sat down in a chair.

"He always has been. Very gifted at it," said Eren, sitting beside me. He started piling his plate full of food.

I turned to the food and chose some type of potato-cheesy thing, macaroni and cheese and cubes of green jello. I was going for comfort food. I tasted the mac and cheese and found it was the best I'd eaten in my entire life. Made with sharp cheddar not that crappy orange American cheese. Yum. And some bacon on the side. There was a plate of something blue, purple and lumpy which smelled fishy. I passed on that one.

Eren went for some crawfishy looking thing, several slices of roasted beast with carrots and potatoes, sauteed greens with beets and onions. He plopped a few spoonfuls of something red and squishy on his plate as well, I didn't ask, since I didn't want to know. Hell had some really bizarre food. He topped it off with foamy, dark beer from a pitcher.

After a few minutes of stuffing food in my mouth and barely tasting it, I finally found the nerve to ask him what no one seemed to be talking about. "What exactly is this war about? Why did they attack us?"

He paused mid-bite and looked at me in astonishment. Putting his fork down, he said, "I forgot that you just got here. It's a very long story, but I'll give you the short version. You realize that gods and goddesses have always had rivalries?"

I nodded my head, while eating more of the salty cheese and potatoes.

He continued, "Most of the time rivalries are kept at a dull roar. But as the human population grows and the dead increase, so have the problems. They are beginning to encroach on our world, pushing us into smaller spaces. The Underworld is not infinite. And it's being filled up with human dead who can't figure out why they're not in heaven or whatever afterlife they envisioned and who refuse to reincarnate to make more space. For a long time Hades, Pluto, Lucifer and Hecate and dozens of other Underworld deities shared the space and divided up the population evenly. They played nicely. But as the pressure increased those niceties fell apart. Divisions started, alliances were formed and political wrangling began. The problems have been going on for a couple thousand years now. It just got bigger when Zeus joined in." He drank his beer.

"Why did Zeus join in?" I asked.

"Well, he's always had a problem with women, treating them as equals. He and Hecate were lovers once. They may even have had a child together, neither will say. When he took power from the Titans, the pre-Greek gods, he allowed Hecate to keep her power. But he never saw her as an equal. I'm guessing Zeus figured out how much he underestimated her and is unhappy about her alliance with Lucifer, who's also very powerful. It's a very strong partnership, politically. A major threat to Zeus, so he banded Pluto, Hades and Arawn together to fight us. But this is the first time Zeus has stepped into the alliance visibly, we always suspected he was part of it."

"So, it's a turf fight?"

"Basically, yes," said Eren.

"Are we going to lose?"

"Who's to say?" he said.

"I am," said Lucifer, who I realized was sitting across from us and had been listening for some time. He swirled a doughnut around his index finger, occasionally taking bites of it. "We're not going to lose, but it's going to get very ugly for a while. In the end, we'll prevail."

"How can you be so sure?" I asked.

"We're smarter. We have learned things as time passed. Zeus is stuck in time, powerful, but he's still living in the ancient Greece of his mind. Pluto's still stuck in old Rome. Hades has a little more brains, as does Arawn." Lucifer slurped down some coffee.

He continued, "We're making allowances for dealing with the human dead, educating them to help with their transition to reincarnation. Their dead have begun to riot against them. We're making strong alliances with other deities of more varied cultures. I think Arawn is their only non-Mediterranean deity. There might be a couple others. We're more diverse and flexible. And we're using modern technology." He smiled and I shuddered. I'd hate to be his enemy.

"I agree," said Eren to me. "We've give them a few battles, so they get greedy and lose their caution. "The next one will set them straight."

I really hoped so. I'd never given war much thought. It had always been present in my life. The Gulf War. Afghanistan, Iraq. Friends of my parents had brothers, fathers, sisters, mothers who fought and sometimes disappeared, never to come home again. Or if they did, they were vastly changed, damaged somehow. It wasn't talked about much in the community. What had affected us most was the weather. Would it frost at just the right time--not too early, not too late to get ice wine? Would there be enough hot, sunny days for a good crop of grapes or would there be too much rain and the grapes would rot on the vine? Or the talk was about TV and who would win American Idol this time. War was way off the agenda.

I finished my dinner with the jello cubes, rolling them around in my mouth, loving the rubbery texture.

"What are you going to volunteer to do?" asked Lucifer, gnawing on a chicken leg.

"I don't know. I'm not really good at anything."

"Why don't you go to the Healers'? They need help and you can find Nuada."

"Can I do that? I thought they'd need people who had skills." I really wanted to find Nuada.

"They need people to just sit and hold patient's hands, get them a glass of water, that sort of thing as well," said Eren.

"I probably need to keep training with Selene, though."

"She'll be busy with Hecate and I for the next couple of days. Strategic planning. I'll tell her you're looking for her though," said Lucifer.

After dinner, even though it was late, I decided to go find the Healers'. I wasn't sleepy, that was nearly all I'd done in the bunker. They might need me, since most of the other folks seemed to be headed to bed.

I walked down the corridors, taking two rights, then a left as Lucifer had told me, but I got lost. All those red and gold, glittery mosaic hallways looked the same. Frustrated, I finally had to get in an elevator, go up to the first floor and ask for directions at the front desk which HellTV mentioned.

The front desk was in a huge lobby and it finally hit me that Lucifer's place was modeled after a glitzy, Vegas Hotel. Breezy fountains full of stone statues of beings I'd never seen, romped above koi ponds. Extravagant artwork filled the three story lobby. And again, the color scheme in red, gold and black. Luscious foliage and fragrant, tropical blossoms added life to everything. The overpowering scent in the room was a tropical flower, maybe tuberose or plumeria.

The Healers' or 'hospital' was a massive room the size of a football field. Someone had told me at dinner that the room usually housed concerts, plays or celebrations. The ceiling was vaulted and filled with sunlight. Several stories underground. No idea how they did it, but the sun felt glorious, warm and uplifting. I hadn't realized how much I missed it.

Most of the patients lay on beds; others sat on couches, either watching TV with headphones or chatting with each other. Dreamy Celtic music played in the background. I could smell lilacs. It didn't feel like the aftermath of a battle. Some of the beds were curtained off by red enclosures. The gold and red theme had taken over this room as well. I wondered if Lucifer recognized any colors besides those and black. It didn't seem so.

There was a desk at the entrance and I went to it. Sitting at the desk and entering data into a computer was a woman, maybe, with an alligator's head and long, long arms. She was dressed in a gold and blue Egyptian looking dress.

"Can I help you," she said, sweetly.

"I've come to volunteer."

"Oh, lovely. I'll call Sasha. He's organizing all our volunteers." She spoke into a cell. "It'll be a few minutes, he's orienting someone at the moment. If you'll just take a seat." She pointed to a waiting area behind me.

I sat down and thumbed through a magazine called 'Deities

Today' which had photos of Selene and several other deities whom I didn't know. Accompanying articles gave their FAQs and a short interview.

After half an hour, Sasha, a tall, muscled blonde with a Russian accent showed up and determined I'd be useful. He showed me around, pointing out the aisle letters and bed numbers which would help me identify a patient. Things were more organized than I thought.

He gave me a phone and showed me the emergency numbers and explained who to call and for what. Then he sent me to bed G8, a woman who had lost an arm.

Feeling a little nervous I sat down. She was still asleep, but I was supposed to sit and wait as her meds were decreased by the machine. She'd wake soon. Beautiful, with reddish, blonde hair, she looked not much older than me. Her chart said she carried some human, some immortal blood, so she would recover quickly. Her name was Olwen.

I flipped through a newspaper, *Life in Hell*, sitting on the table beside her. It gave details of the battle and a list of the dead.

I glanced at Olwen to find green eyes staring at me. "You're awake. How are you feeling?"

"I hardly know. Where am I?" she asked, weakly.

"We're at Lucifer's place. Hell. You're safe."

She lay back and closed her eyes, "No, I'm not."

"I don't understand," I said.

"I was fighting for Arawn," she said, opening her eyes.

"Ah."

"Do you know what happens to prisoners?" she asked, fear widening her eyes.

"No," I said, "I'm new here."

"We are tortured and then killed."

"It doesn't seem like they'd waste energy taking care of you just to torture and kill you. Wouldn't they just dump you in a prison cell somewhere and let you bleed? It would only be part of the torture." I wondered if they really would torture her.

She looked at me skeptically.

"I'll call a healer and let them know you're awake." I pressed the contact number on the cell. When a voice answered I said, "Olwen in bed G8 is conscious."

The husky voice on the other end said, "I'll send someone."

A few uncomfortable minutes later a man came over. It was the gorgeous guy I'd seen in the hallway when I arrived. The one who made me feel so safe and peaceful. He nodded at me and held out his hand, "I'm Nuada."

# CHAPTER TWELVE

I SHOOK HIS HAND. I could feel my face growing warm, then hot. Golden eyes, brown hair, Nuada. "That Nuada?"

"Yes, I'll explain later," he said, smiling.

I nearly fainted from embarrassment. He was the dog Nuada? The dog who'd hung out with me, like forever? The dog I'd whispered all my fears and sadness to? The dog I'd undressed in front of and slept with? I felt sure the color of my face matched Lucifer's walls. I couldn't even look at Nuada. What did he think of me? Who was he really? I shoved all my thoughts, questions and conflicted feelings down deep inside. I'd deal with them later, when we were alone.

He sat down near Olwen and began to talk to her. He asked how she felt. Her ribs and her missing arm ached. She spoke as if her arm was still attached. He told her it was gone. At first she looked shocked, then nodded, tears running down her face.

He unhooked her from the machine and stood over her, moving his hands an inch or so above her body. They hovered around her ribs and shoulders. Nuada looked lit up from the inside. He literally glowed.

I did an experiment and went to that place where I moved the magic out through a sword or arrow. It was then that I could see the energy flowing in streams through his hands and into her body. I could see white rivers moving through veins and along capillaries and into cells. They moved into bones, knitting them together. He moved other things around as well, which seemed to help her relax and not be in as much pain.

I looked around and found I could see what other healers were doing as well. Mostly they seemed to be using a whitish energy, but in a couple places the magic was definitely blue and it looked cooling. A couple of healers had a reddish cast to their energy. I wondered if each one could do all those, or if the color was linked to that healer.

Nuada seemed to have finished and was speaking with Olwen again. She looked more relaxed.

"What will happen to me?" she asked.

"You will heal and go on with your life."

"No, that's not what I mean. Am I a prisoner or can I go home?"

"I will ask someone in charge to inquire about you. I'm simply a healer. But there were no special instructions and there is no guard on you. Whatever choice you make, heal first." He spoke into the cell for a while. When he finished, he said to her, "Someone will come to speak to you soon."

He turned to leave and saw me standing there. "I can't talk to you right now, there is so much to be done. I will meet you later and explain."

I nodded, not knowing what to say. He touched my arm and then left. A warm glow spread through me, although I wasn't sure if it was from his healing touch or just his touch. I went and sat back near Olwen, offering her some water which she drank, gratefully, then she dozed off again.

I busied myself reading the newspaper. I didn't want to think about my own life. While reading I discovered that the Underworld was a much more complicated place than I had realized. It operated much like the rest of earth, except that there was no money. People worked at what they were skilled at, ate, slept, had family or not, argued with their neighbors and read, painted, made music, watched TV. Someone had to do the laundry, cooking and cleaning just like at home. There were large chunks of land where crops were tended, livestock kept. So that's what it's like to be dead.

Just like real life. Unless you reincarnated. Then it was back to real life. Only your actions really, really mattered there. In the real world, life held a much bigger price for failure. And kids were involved there. If you were dead you couldn't have kids. I'd always loved kids. They were so much cooler than adults.

After while Lucifer walked in and said, "How's the patient?"

"When she's awake, she's worried."

"About what?" he asked.

"About being tortured and killed."

He rolled his eyes. "That's so old school. We don't do that any more, although the other side does. It's much more effective to kill our enemies with kindness."

He slid into the chair beside her bed and touched her remaining arm.

Olwen woke with a start, then recognized him and looked more afraid.

"Aah, I see you recognize me," he said, crossing his legs at the knee and then his wrists on top of them. He looked harmless.

She nodded, covering up her fear.

"I know you're afraid of being tortured. We do not do that. When you are well again, we shall offer you a choice. Amnesty, or if you wish it, you may leave and return to Arawn."

She looked at him disbelievingly.

Lucifer sighed and asked, "Why is it that no one ever believes me?"

I laughed.

He said, "It is true. You will not be tortured by *us*. We leave that for Zeus' minions. Take your time and heal." He patted her on the arm, then got up. "Well, ta ta. I've got places to go, things to do, people to see." And he slipped out, disappearing behind another enclosure.

Olwen stared at the space he'd occupied for a minute or so, then asked, "Was he serious?"

Was he ever serious? I wasn't sure. "I've only been here a few days and I don't know him very well, but I'd say, yes."

She nodded, then went back to sleep. I wondered what it would be like to fight in a battle, get knocked out and wake up without an arm. I'd feel awful.

I went back to reading the paper again, found an editorial by Mark Twain. It was very funny, although I didn't get all the jokes I'm sure. Lots of political jabs. I realized with a shock that anyone who died and had not reincarnated could be down here. I could meet anyone! That thought was overwhelming. Who did I want to meet? All the dead writers I'd read? Musicians? My mind drew a blank. Except for one person. I wanted to see Chris. Was he here?

The next thing I knew there was a hand on my shoulder and I found myself face first on the newspaper, drooling. I'd fallen asleep just sitting there.

One of the healers, a tall, thin silver-haired man looked at me and said, "It's time to go to your room and get some sleep, child."

I glanced at Olwen, still asleep.

He said, "She'll be fine, she will sleep for hours yet."

I stood and staggered off towards my room. After a couple of wrong turns, I found it.

I peeled off my clothes, found some PJ's and fell into bed.

Several hours later I woke to a banging noise on my door. My first thought was that I'd overslept for school and Mom was trying to wake me up. When I could open my eyes, I remembered where I was.

I weaved to the door and opened it. Selene stood there, looking radiant as usual. "You look awful," she said, walking into my dark room. She snapped her fingers and a table light went on. "Hecate was worried about you, since no one has seen you since just after the battle."

"Lucifer has seen me. Eren has seen me."

"Ah well, we haven't seen much of either of them. Everyone's busy. Are you okay?"

"I was in a coma when you knocked, that's all. Got to bed really late, or early, I don't know."

"What were you up to, so 'late or early'?"

"I was at the Healers' attempting to be helpful. Eren and Lucifer said I should try working there."

"Aah. So you saw Nuada?"

"Yes," I said, "But I don't understand. I thought he was a dog. Now he's not. I didn't get a chance to talk to him."

"I think I'll leave it to him to explain." She continued, "Go back to sleep and after you've eaten, come to the War Room on level 13 to talk to Hecate and me. We need to get back to your training."

I nodded. She snapped out the light and let herself out. I wobbled back to bed and unconsciousness.

After sleeping for hours I searched for the War Room on level 13. The vertigo was bothering me again. It didn't feel horrible, but it wasn't helpful either. I sure couldn't make any quick moves without leaving part of myself several steps behind.

I got stopped several times by guards, men with animal heads, Anubis, a hawk headed man, a boar headed man and a lion headed man. They told to go right and then right again and then left or something like that. Finally, a gazelle headed man led me to the right place. Clearly the whole building was designed as a maze.

I entered and found Hecate and Selene before a panel of screens.

I cleared my throat. They looked up and Hecate said, "Angelica, how nice to see you." She swiveled her chair around, rocking it back and putting her feet up on the coffee table between us. She wore a T-shirt, jeans and knee-high black boots with no heels. I was astonished by her appearance. Her hair was tied up in a ponytail. She looked nothing like a goddess, except for the power emanating from her.

Selene wore blue leggings and a tunic with a silver choker around her neck, from which dangled a crescent moon. White sandals were slipped over her feet and her hair was braided into a million tiny braids. I wondered if she did it herself or had it done. It must have taken forever.

"Hi," I managed to mumble.

"Pull up a chair," Hecate said, motioning to the vacant chairs by the table.

I sat down, feeling like I was at the principal's office.

"We need you to finish your training quickly and leave," she said

I felt like someone hit me. I was being kicked out. I nodded. This was unexpected.

"Life here is only going to get more dangerous. The war has been amped up by the enemy. Everyone who lives here is either immortal or they are dead. We have all been around for a long time. You, however have only been alive for sixteen years. If you were killed, it would be a tragedy. It is not worth the risk."

All I could hear was that they didn't want me. And suddenly I wanted to stay. Why is it that things work that way? Finally, I worked up the nerve to ask the question which had been burning inside me since I'd read that article by Twain.

"Is my brother here?"

They looked at each other.

"No, we checked when you first arrived. He has never been here."

"So that means what?" I thought I already knew the answer.

Hecate stared into my eyes and asked, "Are you sure you want to know?"

"Yes."

"He's either with Hades or he has reincarnated."

I sunk into the chair. There was no chance I'd see Chris. It hadn't been much of a hope anyway.

"It was foolish for Archimedes to have brought you here. Humans do not come here unless they're dead," said Hecate. "It's never been safe. And Archimedes is certainly not safe around young women like you."

"Why?"

"He was never quite right, even when he was alive. But dead, he has no boundaries against torturing and abusing the young. You are still unharmed only because Lucifer has kept him busy and set guards around you."

"I've never seen any guards."

"No, you aren't able to see them, I'd guess. When I stole you, I left you in Nuada's care."

"But Nuada's only a healer."

Hecate and Serene doubled over with laughter. They nearly stopped and then looked at me and started laughing again.

I crossed my arms and glared at them. "Ha ha ha. Some joke. Why don't you tell it to me?"

"I'm sorry," said Hecate. "I really needed that." She wiped tears from her face. "My dear, healing is only one of Nuada's gifts. He's a Celtic God of Sun, the Sea, Healing, Love and War. Pretty much everything. He's also a great warrior and was a powerful King."

"So why was he a dog?"

"He came to me and said he'd spent too much of his time in arrogance. He thought he needed to learn humility. So I turned him into a dog."

"Isn't there an easier way to learn?" I asked.

"There are other ways to learn, I'm not sure if one is easier than another. But to spend time being an animal is a humbling experience. Deities become so full of themselves, thinking they are superior to everyone. Then they turn into small-minded creatures like Zeus. Becoming an animal allows one to see the divinity in all life, the simplicity and good in all of us."

"Even Archimedes?"

"Even him. His goodness has been twisted and warped. And because he was a brilliant man, he spent eons not being held accountable for his actions. He and Zeus would make a fine pair. But, that's neither here nor there. The question is what are we going to do with you?"

"The vertigo has returned," I said.

"I would assume that. You are simply swimming with magic." She sat back in her chair and looked at me. "What would you like to do?"

"I don't know. I can't function on earth like this. I like it here. I'm worried about Mom. I don't want her to worry about me and I don't know how much time has passed since I came here. I don't know how I'll be able to explain myself when I get back."

Selene said, "If you are killed here during a battle, you would not be able to return home. Ever."

"Would I be here permanently if I died?"

"Unless you reincarnated back to earth," said Hecate.

I nodded.

"What would you gain from staying here longer?" asked Selene.

"I'd like to get this magic straightened out. Get rid of the vertigo. But I like it here."

"Why?" asked Hecate.

"On earth I don't have any friends. No one at school talks to me. I used to have Chris and Mom and Dad. But since I shot Chris, he's gone. Dad hates me and Mom's always too busy putting food on the table to spend time with me."

"But you've spent most of your time here in the Underworld alone," said Selene.

"Not all of it. I've talked to you two and Lucifer and Eren. And Nuada's been with me. Not a great conversationalist, but he's been present. I haven't even had a pet since I was little and our cat got eaten by coyotes. Mom hates animals."

Hecate nodded. "You've been too much alone in the world. I think you should continue volunteering with the Healers' when you are not training. I need Selene here, but you should go to the training grounds every day and do some work. Scathach will assist you. She is an amazingly skilled teacher."

I took a deep breath of relief. My life was changing and I wanted to keep doing all this. I didn't want to go back to my old miserable one. And working at the Healers' was fascinating. If I could learn to actually help there that would be wonderful.

"Well, it's time we got back to work," said Hecate.

"Thank you."

"It's been a pleasure talking to you," said Hecate. "I'll send for you again in a few days to see how you're doing."

I nodded and left the room, making my way to the upper levels and hoping to find some breakfast. When I got to the dining room, I discovered it was lunch time. I was all turned around from being in the bunker during the last battle.

The smells were overwhelming. Rich spices mingled with grilled meats and sweet pastries. I wondered if the dead or immortals worried about getting too fat. Could one taste food after death?

So there I was surveying tables. No one I knew was there, only a few tables had occupants. I wasn't feeling brave enough to sit with complete strangers or courageous enough to go sit with the animal headed guys either. So I sat at a table by myself. A cop-out, but I had a lot on my mind.

While making myself a bacon and egg sandwich, I went over

what Hecate had told me. Chris wasn't here. He might not even be with Hades. He might be some new baby in Wichita, Kansas for all I knew. If he was with Hades then chances are the only place I'd see him would be on the battlefield and I didn't think Hecate was going to let me anywhere near one. For which I felt grateful.

I had just stuffed a big bite of sandwich in my mouth when I felt a light touch on my shoulder and looked up to find Nuada.

"May I join you?" he asked.

I nodded, too full of food to speak. I felt like a pig.

"I wished there had been time to speak with you last night, but there was so much to be done." He looked weary, circles hung under his eyes. His hair was haphazardly pulled back into a leather thong.

I could only nod, my mouth still stuffed full.

He continued. "I wasn't quite sure how to tell you that I was not really a dog. My power of speech was gone, until Hecate transformed me back to what I am."

I finally swallowed and said, "She could have told me."

"Ah, but then I wouldn't have gotten the full impact of what a dog's life is about. However, I'm sure being your beast is much more pleasant than say Eren's."

I blushed, not sure what he was talking about, but feeling that it must have included the long baths and undressing. No boy had ever seen me naked, except maybe Chris, by accident.

"I just wanted to apologize for my part in this. When I went to Hecate, I had no idea you would appear in the Underworld and certainly not that I would be assigned to help you, but it was a pleasure. How are you feeling?"

"The magic isn't under control yet. The training was helping, but since the battle began...." I squirmed under his stare. His gaze seemed to penetrate me.

"Yes, I see now that I look." He took a slab of meat and some carrots and greens and put them on his plate. "Will you start training again?"

"Yes, today. But I'm still really tired. I'm also supposed to go to the Healers' again, so I think I'll do that first."

"Good. Olwen was asking about you. I think you'll be good

company for her."

I felt more uneasy and decided to put the attention back on him. "What about you? Do you spend your time only at the Healers'?"

"When I'm not sleeping or eating. At least after a battle. Although I think this is the first chance I've had to really eat a meal since it started. And only catnaps when I couldn't stand anymore. Healing takes its toll even for us gods."

"What will happen next?"

His golden eyes were really spectacular, warm. They made me feel warm.

"Oh, battles in the Underworld are very civilized. We've got all the time in the world. It's our turn to attack. Likely they're licking their wounds, they had more casualties than we did. This next one might be a deciding battle. But then I'm sure the other side thought the last one would be since they brought Zeus in."

"Who are we bringing in to match Zeus?"

"Not who, what. We have technology."

"But won't they have it soon as well?"

No, they've always pooh-poohed technology. I don't think they'll adapt that fast, Zeus, Hades and Pluto aren't open to new ideas. It's why their attrition rate is so high."

"What do you mean?"

"Ever since the war began the brightest of the newly dead tire of their reign and come to our side."

"And you're not concerned with security? With someone stealing battle plans, secrets?"

"Of course we are. We have a huge security system. It's invisible to you, not all of our security forces are human."

I wasn't sure I wanted to know what sort of creatures security employed. Some of the ones I'd seen walking or slithering or flying around were scary enough. Nuada on the other hand was lovely to look at. I couldn't find anything about him that I didn't like. Except maybe that he was a couple thousand years older than me and wouldn't age.

Lucifer slid into a seat across from us. "Ah, if it isn't the Healer and the Healee."

# CHAPTER THIRTEEN

"HELLO LUCIFER," said Nuada, coolly. "Well, I must see if I can get some sleep." He rose from the table and left. He just left as if I was nothing. As if we hadn't just been conversing warmly. As if he hadn't spent the last several weeks following me everywhere.

I was completely baffled and felt let down.

Lucifer was filling a plate full of desserts.

"Don't you ever eat the main dish?" I asked him.

"My body doesn't actually need food," he said. "Angels, even fallen ones don't normally eat. This is simply entertainment."

I shook my head at the strangeness of this world and continued eating.

"A word of caution my dear," he said, biting into a cookie. "You might not want to get too attached to folks down here until you return for good."

"Return for good?"

"You know, dead, ready for the afterlife?"

"Oh."

"Not that we aren't enjoying your company, but it'll make it very difficult for you to return to your life. It's important to truly live while you're still alive. And the Underworld can be a very seductive place."

"And I can't be truly alive here?" I asked, wiping my face with my napkin and pushing my plate away.

"It is possible," he said, eyes gazing off into the distance. "I do remember a case of one young man who found his way here, searching for his lover. He stayed and lived happily. Absolutely fulfilled, but he had no one left on earth. And he didn't want children. Plus, he'd already grown up and taken responsibility for his life."

"And I have my Mom."

"And your father," he said.

"He doesn't care about me. He hates me."

"No, he doesn't hate you. He carries an enormous amount of guilt. Did you ever consider that he feels responsible for your brother's death? He was the adult who left a fourteen year old child *without* supervision and *with* a gun. Had he been around the circumstances might have been very different. I wonder if he doesn't feel as if he pulled the trigger himself."

I felt completely astounded, then stupid, then guilty. Why hadn't I though of that?

"Ah. I see you hadn't considered that possibility. A healthy adult would try to make peace with such a man. I realize you are not yet an adult, but you are nearly there. I am not saying your father has acknowledged any of these feelings, they may just be bubbling around in his psyche and it's possible he might never bring any of them up to his conscious mind. You can't do anything about that. However, I think it's important for you to try to speak with him about the accident and talk about the effects it had on *you*. If he can't hold up his side of the conversation, that's his problem. You will have tried."

My fingernails dug into the palms of my hands. I so didn't even want to talk to Dad. He hadn't talked to me at all since Chris died. Not one word. He'd moved into the winery office and lived there for a year until Mom and I gave up and moved into a new house. Then we moved to Seattle. Somehow I didn't think there would be any forgiveness on his part. Instead of being sad about it, the whole thing just pissed me off.

I raised my voice. "So, you really think I should try to talk to him? Despite the fact he hasn't tried once, to talk to me in two years. He hasn't spoken a word to me since I shot Chris."

"I may be wrong, but I do know that it crushed your heart when your brother died and again when your father rejected you. Your mother hasn't done a decent job of picking up the slack. Her heart's broken and she's ignoring it. Your entire family has shattered and no one is talking about it. Things have been swept under the carpet and everyone soldiers on. I think it would break your parents even more if you disappeared without a trace."

That was something I couldn't believe. My dad hated me and I didn't think that would ever change. He was a stubborn old coot and would never admit he did anything that could have led to Chris' death. Mom, while she loved me, somehow always made me feel as if I were an accessory in her life. Extra baggage. Like a purse which didn't match and had gone completely out of style, but still had a little sentimental value, so she'd stuff it in the back of the closet until she could let it go. I was getting ever closer to being let go.

I told Lucifer all this and he sat thinking about it then said, "So you believe they don't need any resolution with you, to see you grow up and succeed with your life? That is possible, I could believe it of your father, although not your mother. The point is, I think *you* need some resolution from them. I think you need to bring this out into the light, that they haven't forgiven you for your brother's death. That they've completely cut off their love for you. That in all of this they have failed, alienated and lost their only living child. I think once you've done that, and only then, you will be able to truly forgive them and move on with your life."

I sat back and thought about it. That was what an adult should do. And it scared me to death to attempt it. "That's really frightening," I said.

"Why?"

"Because if I have to go back and I bring this up with Mom, she'll probably kick me out. And I'm only sixteen. I'm still in high school. I can't even do anything to support myself."

"I don't think she'll kick you out for telling her the truth about how you feel. She might cut you off emotionally even more, but it seems like she's already done that. At least you would know where you stood." He drank coffee to wash down the doughnut. "And it's high time you made some decisions about the rest of your life and where you're going with it. Collapsing yourself into a relationship with a 2,000 year old God is not the best choice you could make, I think."

"What?" He always astonished me with what he could see. "He's not interested in me."

Lucifer arched an eyebrow and looked at me. "I noticed that chemical thing between the two of you. I see everything that happens in my little chunk of the world. It's my job. I'm not saying a relationship between the two of you would be bad, it's just that you're alive, he's not. You've got some major things in your life that are unresolved. Have you seen those people who at the instant a long term relationship ends rebound directly into another relationship?"

I nodded, thinking about Aunt Molly. Her husband dumped her for a coworker and she jumped into bed with Sam, the next guy who came along. It didn't last long. Sam forgot to tell her he was married and she forgot to ask.

"They never give themselves time to process the first relationship and don't learn anything from it. They don't grow before they leap into the next one and still have to learn the same lesson. People do this again and again. They can't enter fully into the next relationship as an equal because they have too much unfinished business."

"I don't think I can change the way Mom and Dad are."

"Of course you can't. But, I believe you need to find the guts to tell them how you feel about the way they have treated you. Finish things up and come to some sort of resolution, so you can move on, either with them or without them. That's all. It will make you stronger whatever the outcome. Once you've done that processing then you'll be free to enter into a relationship. And take responsibility for the rest of your life. But that's just my take on things after watching humans for a few thousand years. It's a suggestion, not a mandate. Now I know you don't have any experience here, but collapsing into a relationship, any relationship, between consenting adults isn't a healthy choice. Sometimes it works, but it's not healthy." He looked up as Anubis came over and whispered in his ear.

"Thank you," he said, and the dog-headed man bowed and left. Lucifer closed his eyes for a minute or two, smiled and then opened them. "I think this might be interesting to you, care to come along?" he asked me.

"Okay."

He snapped his fingers and I watched in astonishment as the dirty dishes lifted off the table and flew towards the kitchen.

I got up and followed him out of the dining room and down the hallway. He led me down several more corridors until we came to one which opened out into a huge rock cavern lit by torches. There was no mosaic here, but the cave was the size of a huge stadium and the ceiling dripped with stalactites. It was slightly dark here, smoky. The sides of the room were lined with seats like choir risers, each level raised above the others.

"This is our training ground. We normally use it for sparring and training. But we've a huge influx of refugees coming. Deserters from our enemies."

As he spoke, I saw doors opening across from us and people filing in. Lucifer climbed up onto the bleachers, I followed. He stopped about halfway up, where the shadows began, I noticed.

The cavern was slowly filling up with people and creatures. They looked dirty and tired as if it had been an ordeal to get here. Some were carrying or half carrying others and there were stretchers and travois with people on them. A huge, black wolf brought up the rear. When I looked at it, the wolf's red eyes met mine. I shivered and looked away it scared me so much.

Seven healers made their way through the crowd, tending to the worst of the injured. Nuada was not among them. Finally, the doors closed. Everyone was inside.

Lucifer sat watching. I wondered if he was looking for someone. Three people stood apart from the others. Two men and a women. When I closed my eyes, pulled up the magic and looked at the crowd I could see auras around people. Not like all the psychics see auras-- this was different or maybe more pronounced. The auras had texture.

The dead humans were surrounded by what looked like the psychics' aura, maybe they were just more basic. Some of the creatures had slippery, oozy auras about them. Other beings had sharp, jagged auras. The three people had completely different auras. The wolf had a black aura, but I couldn't stand to look at it long.

Of the three, one of the men had a watery blue aura, the other man's aura was brown and pulsed with life. The woman had an almost blinding white aura. She looked straight at us.

Lucifer nodded to her. She spread her arms as if to say, "Well, then help us." Then she bowed, cocking her head to one side. If ever there was a bow which felt sarcastic, that was it.

He laughed and rose walking down into the light where he began speaking, his voice filling the entire cavern.

"Welcome everyone to our little part of the Underworld. Presently the healers will be removing those of you with the worst injuries, please make room for them to do their work. It would be helpful if everyone else would wait here while we assign rooms, and most important dining rooms, to everyone else. Then after you have checked in, you may go to the Healers' or dining rooms, and find your friends, lovers or partners."

He continued, "I know many of you are suspicious as to what your treatment will be here. I assume that should you decide to stay, you have chosen to be part of our side. If that's not the case, then it's time for you to leave now. We are fighting a war here and everyone is expected to do their part. When you are checking in you will be asked where your skills lie. As more people join us we have needs for cooks, healers, farmers and even people who are willing to simply do laundry or clean rooms. Everyone's skills are valued here."

I had stayed up in the shadows and could see the new folks talking between themselves. Some of them hadn't expected this. Had their treatment with Hades been so bad that they'd defected anyway and come here just hoping it would be better? The three leaders still stood clustered together, not speaking. They occasionally nodded at something Lucifer said,

I watched the healers take some of the newcomers out on their stretchers or gurneys. Most of them were unconscious. Or dead.

Permanently. I watched several whose souls became thinner until they vaporized into mist. I knew from my short time at the Healers' that their dead bodies would vanish completely in a few hours. Dying again, once in the Underworld, they lost even the chance to reincarnate. Even the immortal gods and goddesses died this way. Forever.

Lucifer continued talking, "I would like to thank you for having the courage to come here. In the next few days either I or one of my assistants will be coming around to speak with each of you individually, to find out how you're doing. Thank you."

He turned and walked back into the shadows and sat down.

"Who are those three?" I asked.

He looked at me and asked "Why are you interested in knowing only about them?"

I shrugged, "They look different."

"Yes, they do. I didn't know you could see that. They're all Celtic deities. The gentleman with the horns on his head is Cernunnos, he is a God of Fertility, the Underworld and Animals. The one with the armor is Manannan, a Sea God. The lady is Cerridwen. She is a Goddess of the Underworld, Knowledge and Transformation. To have them leave when Arawn is still with Hades and Zeus is a great coup." He smiled so wide, it threatened to wrap around his head.

"Come," he said, "let us go to the Healers'."

We left the bleachers and as we crossed the floor of the cavern, one of the new people left the crowd and moved towards us. It was Cerridwen.

"Lucifer," she said, nodding her head.

"Cerridwen," he said, taking her hand and kissing it.

I vaguely remembered reading about her in *Life is Hell*, and that she was a Crone Goddess. Her hard, dark eyes told me she was no one to mess with.

"Did you mean everything you said?"

"Of course. Life, even mine, is too short to spend it lying. The truth will always come out anyway."

"You know there will be others coming," she said.

"That is what I am hoping."

"Zeus is a tyrant few of us can tolerate."

"I've met him."

"Why are you accompanied by this live human?" she asked, gently, nodding at me.

"Ah, this is our tourist, Angelica. Cerridwen, Angelica, Angelica, Cerridwen. Angelica returned one of us who was trapped in her world. She's become infected by magic which can't be removed and we're trying to help her contain the magic. She is under Hecate's and my own protection."

Cerridwen stared at me questioningly. She had a lot more to ask me, I thought. I wasn't sure if she was friend or enemy. She nodded at Lucifer and returned to the crowd.

"Come, Let's move on," he said.

We walked through curving passage ways. I didn't recognize anything. "Is this the way to the Healers'?"

"Shortcut," he said, grinning.

After five more minutes of hallway, we climbed three stories of very wide stairs which emptied out into the Healers'. Lucifer walked through the room to the opposite side where the greeters desk sat. He asked where the newcomers were.

I followed him as he walked past those beds. Clusters of healers and assistants were around each bed, trying to get people stabilized I'd guess. At the fourth bed, he stopped.

I couldn't see what was happening. There were two healers and three assistants at the bed behind the partial curtain.

"We will wait a couple minutes I think," he said.

I stood and looked around. About ten people had been brought up from the cavern. I wondered if they'd been injured in the battle or in trying to defect. After a few minutes the curtains opened as the healers came out.

"How is he?" asked Lucifer.

"He'll be fine, although we had to amputate his leg below the knee," said a tall, woman with short, black hair. "He will need to be fitted with a prosthetic."

Lucifer nodded. "Can we see him?"

The other healer, a man with long, gray hair nodded.

We went to the bed. Lying in it was Chris. His eyes were closed and his face streaked with dirt. One attendant stood adjusting a blue drip-line attached to his arm. The other sat in a chair watching us.

I stood staring at the him, open mouthed, not knowing what to do. Should I disturb him or not? I looked at Lucifer and he raised his eyebrows at me. Both of the attendants left, I went and sat in the chair and took his hand.

"Chris," I said softly.

His brown eyes opened and looked unfocused at first, then looked at me. "Angie?" he asked, his eyebrows furrowing.

"It's me," I said. "It's good to see you. I'm sorry about shooting you."

"I know, it was an accident." He looked confused. "Are you dead?"

"No, I'm alive."

"But I'm still dead, right?" he asked.

"Yes, you're still dead."

He looked relieved. "Where am I?"

"You're at Lucifer and Hecate's."

"We made it," he said. "What are you doing here if you're not dead?"

"Long story. I'll wait till you're up for it."

"Are you safe?"

"I'm as safe here as anywhere," I said.

Lucifer tapped me on the shoulder. One of the healers had returned. He gave Chris some liquid to sip. When he was done, Chris smiled, put his head back on the pillow and was out.

The healer said, "He needs to sleep for the rest of the day and probably the night. Come back after breakfast tomorrow and he will be awake again."

I nodded and said, "Thank you."

"Well, that was a surprise," said Lucifer, eyeing me coolly.

"What?"

"I hadn't expected your brother to show up here."

"But you knew he was here when you went to the cavern."

"Yes, I know the identity of anyone who enters my domain.

When they came to the mountains that border my section of the Underworld I felt all of them. Sometime before dinner. So I went looking for you."

"What do I do now?"

"Let's see, you have time to put in here and I believe you have an appointment with Scathach. I think you have plenty to keep you busy."

It wasn't what I'd meant and he knew it. It just meant he wasn't going to answer the real question. What would I do now that my brother was here? I didn't really want to return to earth to my cold, cold life, when the only person I really loved and who loved me, was here. At least I think he still loved me. I had after all killed him. Even if it was an accident, I still took his future away from him.

"Well, I must be off. I've got a completely overwhelming schedule," he said, with an affected manner, pronouncing 'schedule' with a 'sh' sound. I often had the feeling that he was much, more dangerous than Hecate, but he hid all his power behind humor. He nodded and walked off behind the row of curtains for the newcomers.

I looked at Chris sleeping. It felt so wonderful to see him again. He had a scar on one arm that was new, but otherwise looked the same. Except he was minus half a leg. There seemed to be no damage to his face or chest where I'd shot him. When you die you get a perfect body back.

After a few minutes I decided to return to the training ground. I was sure that training would entail me wiping up the floor with my body. Selene had beat the crap out of me without even trying. Scathach probably wouldn't be different.

It took at least half an hour, four wrong turns and asking for directions three times before I found it again.

The cavern was filled with warriors sword fighting, practicing bow and arrow against one wall and doing martial arts in another corner. In the very middle of the cave stood one of the newcomers. The God who Lucifer called Manannan. Several of the warriors had stopped fighting and were watching.

Manannan was sparring with someone who wore body armor like him, and a helmet, which he did not. Their legs and arms were bare, but both had shields and swords. His shield was painted with ocean waves and a seabird of some sort. It looked very realistic. The other person's shield had large rocks and green earth painted on it. Manannan's opponent was tall and muscular in a wiry sort of way, where he was shorter and thicker muscled. And the God was getting whupped. I didn't think it was because he was tired from the journey either. The other person was relentless and had a longer reach. Finally, he cried out, "Yield!" and his opponent stopped. They grabbed hands and did that sort of fist bump that guys do.

His opponent pulled off the helmet and I could see a feminine face with short cropped red hair. Was it a woman? They spoke for a few minutes, then Manannan picked up a pack and other gear and walked with a few others towards me and the door. His opponent followed.

He was laughing a deep, belly laugh. It sounded pleasant to hear. He stopped just short of the door and turned to say to his opponent, "I'll be back tomorrow to spank your sorry ass."

She laughed at him. As she came closer, I could tell the gender. Her laugh was almost musical. "No, you'll be back, but things won't turn out the way you thought. It's good to see you old friend."

As he and his followers walked through the door, I could smell sweat and dust. Several of them looked at me strangely as if I was a green alien, I thought.

The woman stopped at the doorway, waved at them and turned to me. "You must be Angelica."

I nodded, nervously.

"Well, I'm Scathach. Let's get started."

# CHAPTER FOURTEEN

I FOLLOWED her into the cavern. On the nearest wall was a door which led to a room filled with weapons and armor. She fitted me with a padded vest and handed me a wooden sword, exchanging her real sword for a wooden one. Then we went back out into the cavern.

"Why are you putting that sword back in with all the others? Don't you have a special sword that's just yours?"

"The choice of weapon is important, what is more crucial is what you do with it. I have no weapons of my own, except this knife. I use what is nearby. I always tell my students, don't get attached to the weapon, focus on improving your own skill. I know it is not your intent to become a warrior, but to learn how to use your magic and make it flow more smoothly. However, since we are in a war here, I will help you learn how to defend and attack as well."

She picked an open spot near a side wall and started at the beginning with me. Selene had taught me some of this, but she had focused more on magic. Scathach taught me how to stand and move, where my balance should be at any given point. It was like dancing, which I wasn't great at either. But she pointed out that in formal dancing one is mostly following someone else's steps, not just following the music and moving your body where it wants to go. In fighting the music is all the people around you and you need to move your body in concert with their actions. It's a collaboration.

So we danced around and she whacked me again and again with her wooden sword. I knew I'd be covered with bruises. After an hour of this, my arm turned to rubber and I was drenched with sweat. I felt useless.

"You've had enough for today," she said. "Come back tomorrow."

I returned the sword, threw the vest in the laundry bin and staggered back to my room. After showering I grabbed lunch, or was it dinner, and went to the Healers'. Chris was still asleep. They sent me to spend time with Olwen.

She looked much better. Her color was brighter and she was awake.

"Hello, how are you today?" I asked.

"Fine." She looked confused.

"I'm Angelica. I was here yesterday when you woke up."

"Oh, I remembered your face, but not from where. Why are you here?"

"Everyone who is here in this part of the Underworld must volunteer for a job. For some reason they thought I should work at the Healers', just sitting with people and talking. No idea why. It's not like I'm a great conversationalist."

Olwen looked at me with her head tilted, as if I'd said something strange. "But you're still alive," she said.

"Yes, I am."

"Why?"

"Oh, why am I here if I'm still alive." I said.

She nodded.

"I broke a mirror to let someone out of it, then got infected with more magic than I could handle. The guy who I rescued brought me here and they can't remove the magic, so they're trying to teach me how to use it. Right now that involves beating me senseless with wooden swords." I showed her the blisters I was getting on my hand.

She laughed.

"So how did you get here?" I asked.

She looked at me for a full minute before speaking. "One minute

I was in the middle of battle, somewhere behind Arawn. The next someone sliced off my sword arm and I fell. All I could think about was getting to the edge of the field so I wouldn't be trampled. Then I woke up here with my arm missing."

"I'm sorry."

"I only wish my missing arm would stop hurting."

"I remember when I was ten, I fell and broke my leg. Even though it was in a cast and I couldn't walk on it for weeks, I had dreams of running."

She nodded. "I have been having dreams of braiding flowers using both hands."

"Is there anyone you know here?"

"No. Why would there be?"

"We've had a few defectors from Hades and Arawn. I just wondered if you knew any of them."

"No one has come. They won't let me wander around without anyone; they're afraid I might fall and I don't feel strong enough yet."

"They must have a list of the newcomers around. I'll see if I can find one for you," I got up and went to ask the reception desk. I spotted Nuada leaving a bed with a tent around it, he nodded at me, looking grim.

At the desk I was handed a print out of the newcomers, which I took back to Olwen. When I got to her bed I saw Cerridwen sitting in one of the chairs.

They stopped speaking and looked at me as I entered.

"I found a list of the new arrivals."

They didn't respond.

"Would you like me to leave?" I asked.

Cerridwen raised an eyebrow and looked at Olwen. Olwen said, "No, please stay. Cerridwen was just telling me of their journey here."

Cerridwen gave me a slightly suspicious look and continued, "We were in the pass when we were ambushed. I recognized only one of our attackers, O'Gara."

"Ah, one of Lugh's people."

"Yes, if Lucifer's forces had not come, we would have been slaughtered."

"So Arawn is keeping people from leaving."

"He was very angry you could not be found. He always had a soft spot for you."

I was shocked, this young woman before me must be a Goddess. I hadn't seen it before. Her aura still wasn't as strong as Cerridwen's, but it was more noticeable than yesterday. It was yellow and filled with white daisies. I'd have to look her up on the computer when I went back to my room

"Well, I am not going back. I have been treated only with kindness since coming here. I cannot say the same of Hades' hospitality. Or of Arawn's."

I sat and looked at the readout. Chris' name was on it and surprisingly I recognized a few others, Houdini, Alastair Crowley and Arthur Conan Doyle (no Sir listed). I sat and pondered all the amazing dead people I could meet when Nuada entered.

"Good afternoon," he said, taking in all the occupants of the room.

"Nuada!" cried Cerridwen and rose to hug him.

I hadn't pictured her as much of a hugger. She looked too formidable.

"Cerridwen. I am so happy to see you. I didn't know you were one of the defectees. I've been so busy helping the injured," said Nuada.

"How long have you been here?" asked Cerridwen.

"Since I left Earth. Hecate has always been a teacher for me."

"Yes, she is astonishing. I remember her from before this long war, but I have not seen her yet," said Cerridwen.

"I believe she is keeping busy elsewhere. Lucifer is the one who comes to the Healers'."

"He's a strange creature," she said, looking at me, "I do not mean to offend. He puzzles me."

"He puzzles me too," I said.

Nuada said, "He is not what he seems and he sees everything, too much for my taste. And if he doesn't like what he sees, he has no qualms about telling you about it."

I wondered what he'd talked to Nuada about. What had Nuada done?

"Is that how you see him?" Cerridwen asked me.

"Oh, yeah. He's nailed me to the wall a few times already and I haven't been here long. But he's been right about most of it I think."

"But not all?" she asked.

"There are gray areas. It's about my life and what he thinks I should do. I'm not sure he's right. I'm not sure action on my part will make a difference." I was thinking about his comments about talking to Dad.

Cerridwen nodded. "How is it that you are here and still alive?"

I told her my story. She seemed intrigued and asked, "Will you stay here or return to earth?"

"I don't know. It's unclear if I can control the magic. I don't know if I'll be allowed to stay."

"Your future is uncertain then. That is as it should be. It's unhealthy to know too much about one's future," she said.

Nuada laughed. I looked at him questioningly and he said, "Cerridwen is especially gifted at seeing into the future."

She said, "It's one thing to look into the future of others and tell them just enough to help them achieve their dreams. It's quite another to gape at all your own possibilities laid out in front of you."

We watched Nuada examine Olwen. She had been out of bed and walking around with another person for support quite a bit yesterday.

"I think I will clear you to go to your room. You've already been checked in. You'll need to come here once a day for at least a week so we can make sure everything's healing properly. But we need your bed."

Olwen looked delighted.

"Angelica can show you to your room."

I asked, "Why do you need her bed?"

"There are more defectees coming. Another group has been sighted near the South pass. Lucifer has sent help for them, because Hades and Arawn attacked the runaways."

# CHAPTER FIFTEEN

"IS THERE room for all of them?" I wondered aloud.

"Oh yes, Lucifer creates room and resources. He's a master at that."

Olwen and Cerridwen had gathered up the few things which belonged to Olwen. I walked beside her, in case Olwen had any problems, but she seemed to be doing fine. Her room was just down the hall from mine and I told her if she needed help or company to call me.

I left the two of them chatting away and went to my room. My shift at the Healers' was over. I felt too tired to eat and fell in bed with my clothes on, wondering at the changes this place was making in me. I would never have been forward enough to make such an invitation, back in my old life.

The next few days settled into a pattern. Breakfast, I often ate with Olwen. Then a workout with Scathach, who I learned was something less than a goddess, more than human. The computer entry said she might be Sidhe or Fey. What was perfectly clear was her ability to train warriors. I was getting into shape and receiving a few less bruises every day. Then a shower, lunch and time spent at the Healers'. Then maybe dinner or collapsing into bed.

Chris still had not become conscious. The healers weren't

particularly concerned. They said he had a head injury in addition to the amputation and needed sleep to heal. They said they'd let me know as soon as he woke up. Still, I sat by his bed whenever I could, and talked to him and held his hand. And waited.

The next group of refugees arrived. Twice as many as before. I wondered how long this would go on before Hades and company simply attacked here. I was curious about a great many things by the time Hecate called me in again.

We sat in the war room again. Selene wasn't there.

"Scathach tells me you're progressing well."

I snorted with laughter.

"All right, you're progressing," she said.

"That's more accurate. I have less bruises anyway."

"You realize she's trained some of the greatest warriors of all time?"

"Well, I'm certainly not one of them."

"No, that is not your fate," she said.

"What is my fate?" I asked.

"I'm not sure. Right now it seems to be in flux. It's still mutable."

"That's pretty vague."

She put her bare feet up on the coffee table and leaned back, crossing her arms behind her head. "What would you like your fate to be?"

"I want to live happily ever after."

"Doing what?"

"I'm not sure. I never saw myself being the happy homemaker type. I wanted kids, but not to be a stay at home Mom. I've never been in love, although I've definitely been in lust. Not enough to make the first move though. I love reading and listening to music, but you can't make a living doing that. So far, I think I'm probably just a boring teenager."

"With magic oozing out of her every pore," she said.

"Yeah, that too. I am enjoying working at the Healers' though. I've learned so much and I love watching a healer work. They're amazing."

The door opened and Lucifer slid inside. He sat on the couch, his face wrinkled with worry.

Hecate asked, "What's wrong?"

Lucifer looked up, almost in shock, as if he hadn't noticed we were there. "I'm trying to decide whether someone is telling the truth."

"Who?"

"Morrigan."

Hecate's eyes widened. "She is here?"

"Yes, she came with the last group of refugees. Disguised as a wolf."

Hecate looked down at her hands. "I felt a major power enter, but I hadn't imagined her."

Lucifer said, "She is here and says that Arawn wants to come, provided he's given immunity."

"That has been our policy thus far, but Arawn...," said Hecate, putting her hand to her chest. She was clearly disturbed by this development.

"Yes, I know. He's caused so much damage. Yet, gaining him and the rest of his people would certainly shift the power in our direction."

"If he's not a Trojan horse," said Hecate.

"*If*," said Lucifer. "Or *if* Morrigan's not a Trojan horse. Or Cerridwen."

"Cerridwen I can vouch for," said Hecate. "I know her well enough to know that if she's here, then she's with us."

"The other thing is, I think we need to attack soon. The longer we wait, the more time they have to build a defense."

"But that's exactly what they expect, for us to turn right around and attack them. The waiting is making them sweat. I know Hades and Zeus. Sitting around waiting to be attacked will drive them crazy."

"But are you sure they won't just attack us again, not wait for us to take our turn?" asked Lucifer.

"I really don't think they will. They haven't in a thousand years of war."

"But what if all the defections change that?" he asked.

"I don't think they will, but if they do we're ready for that," said Hecate. "We've been all through this."

"I know, I just worry."

Hecate smiled at him. "I'm more worried about Morrigan and Arawn. Can we trust either of them? I'll meet with Morrigan. In the training ground. I'd like Cerridwen there. And Nuada. Perhaps on the pretense of watching Angelica train. Cerridwen can tell me if Morrigan is being truthful," said Hecate.

"But even if she is, there's no guarantee Arawn is being truthful with her," said Lucifer.

"No. However it's very difficult to lie to Morrigan. I can't believe he has the skill to pull it off."

"I can. Zeus and Hades may have taught him a thing or two," said Lucifer.

"I'm not sure they can bring his power level up though. I'm not sure there's any way he could increase his power that much. To compete with her?"

"You may be right," he said.

"Would you like to be present while I discuss him with her?"

"I would like to be absent while she's around. She terrifies me," said Lucifer.

This astonished me. Lucifer terrified? What kind of creature was Morrigan?

"As she should. She sees into all of our darkest places and reflects them back at us," said Hecate.

I didn't want to be around her either if that was the case.

Lucifer looked at me and asked, "To change the subject to something cheerier, how are you doing, my dear?"

"Okay." I was thinking, here he goes again. On the attack.

"Your brother hasn't woken up yet, has he?"

I shook my head.

"So you have no idea what you're going to do?"

I said, "No. Are you trying to get rid of me?"

"Au contraire. I quite enjoy your company. It's nice to speak with someone who hasn't been around a thousand years and doesn't think they have all the answers," he said.

"Good, because I have a very limited amount of answers."

"So, you're training with Scathach? And working with the healers?"

"Yup."

"Anything else happening?"

"Not really, should there be?"

"I just wondered how that crush was going."

I felt horrified. How did he know? "What crush?" I asked, covering up as best I could.

He laughed and said, "You know what crush."

Hecate stared at me. "Well, I don't know what crush. Tell me," she said to Lucifer.

"You know. Nuada."

I covered my face to hide the fact that it was burning red.

"Nuada," she said, softly. I could almost see her cocking her head in interest. "Well, I hadn't anticipated that. That does complicate things."

"Oh please," I said. "He hardly knows I exist."

"More than hardly, I'd say," said Lucifer.

"She's just his type. Thin, dark hair, stunning eyes and lips. And he's seen inside her and loves her kindness and thoughtfulness," said Hecate.

"Yeah, loner, loser and laughable," I said.

Lucifer howled with laughter at that. Hecate just looked more thoughtful, which really worried me.

"Okay," I said, getting up. "Time for me to go meet Scathach. I think she has more bruises to give me."

Hecate said, "Expect an audience."

I cringed.

"And I think I'll have Cerridwen begin working with your magic. Selene is too busy with our war effort. I want you to keep progressing. Cerridwen will be an excellent teacher. You're not always going to be able to whack someone to keep your magic under control. Wars do end."

I nodded and left, still feeling embarrassed. I hadn't even admitted to myself how I felt about Nuada. I'd never dated. Ever. No one wanted to be seen with me. I had no idea how to handle an attraction like this. For a God, no less. It seemed like a good idea to just bury the whole thing and enjoy the eye candy. Maybe that's all it was.

Later that day at the training grounds, Scathach whacked me in the ribs. "You're not paying attention."

I refocused my thoughts to my body. Breathing, balance and flow. Pay attention to what she's doing. I feinted right and stabbed under her chin, catching her with the wooden sword.

"Better. But remember that's an awful small target, better to slice than stab around the neck area. You're likely to cause more damage there. Okay, break."

I nodded and stopped, bent over to breathe. On one side of the room far up on the bleachers sat Olwen, Cerridwen and Nuada. Their energy felt focused on the other side where Morrigan and Hecate were speaking quietly. I could feel everyone's power swirling around the cavern. The Morrigan/Hecate side seemed so power heavy it felt as if that portion of the cave would sink into the earth.

Lucifer was right. Morrigan was frightening. Just knowing she existed made me shiver.

# CHAPTER SIXTEEN

I COULD FEEL her creepiness without looking. She exuded death in a cold, foggy, graveyard, middle of the night sort of vibe. Except worse than I ever could have imagined. And I have a great imagination. This was even more visceral. I felt as if the life was draining from my body. That was the last rational thought I had before my face hit the ground.

I woke to find myself lying on a bleacher, surrounded by Cerridwen, Olwen, Nuada and Scathach.

"Don't move," Cerridwen said. She held my head in her hands, warm, comforting hands.

"I wasn't going to."

"What was happening before you passed out?" asked Nuada. I felt energy flowing through my body. He was moving his hands about an inch above me.

"I was thinking of Morrigan, I felt like my life was being leeched out of me." I trembled.

"Stop!" he said. "Think of spring, the new growth of trees, the sun shining, the earth coming back to life."

I imagined wildflowers in bloom, the smell of sagebrush and the heat of the sun after winter snow.

"Good," said Cerridwen.

I felt better, warmer.

She removed her hands from my head and gently lay my head on the bench. Nuada stopped moving his hands and said, "I think you can sit up when you feel like it."

I sat up. Hecate and Morrigan were gone. "How long was I out?"

"Not long," said Olwen.

"You should not be near her. She is not compatible with the living and you are still very much alive," said Cerridwen.

I nodded.

"You definitely should not be thinking about her," said Nuada.

"As if I have control over where my brain goes," I said.

"Well, then we must work on that," said Cerridwen. "Come, let's get you some food."

Scathach said, "We're done for today."

I took off my padded vest and Scathach took it along with my sword, which lay where we'd been working.

Nuada left to return to the Healers'. Cerridwen and Olwen took me to my room, where I showered and changed. Then we went to the dining room.

I ladled up some amazing vegetable beef soup. And ate wonderful rolls.

Cerridwen ate a sandwich while watching me. Olwen kept the conversation going almost by herself. She was amazed by everything here, from the lights disguised as torches, to the mosaic walls to the fabulous food. It made me wonder what the rest of the Underworld was like.

I faced the door and noticed Lucifer enter, more casually than usual. He sat next to Eren and took a roll off the serving plate. Then he said something to Eren, who looked momentarily alarmed, then masked his shock. It was replaced by a grim look as he nodded. Lucifer ate the roll in one bite and caught me looking at him. He nodded and walked out of the room, his wings fluttering, almost nervously.

A few minutes later Eren got up and went to three different tables and each time spoke quietly to a man at the table. Each one got the same grim look on their face. Then Eren left. A few minutes later, one man left. Then after a pause, the next one went. After while, the third man slipped out of the room.

Cerridwen saw me watching them and said, "The next battle is about to start."

"How can you tell?"

"I have the gift of seeing."

"What does that mean?" I asked.

"I can see people's intent, events that will happen."

"Who will win?" I asked.

"That is not clear. What I see are big events like the battle. Streaming out from it are many possible outcomes. Everything hinges on the individual actions of several people."

"So if you could affect the action of those individuals you can determine who wins?"

"Perhaps. But in order to affect someone's action, I would have to put myself in that time stream. Which could change everything. Unforeseen actions of other individuals may come in to play. The future is a complex dance and to have the hubris to meddle with it is foolish." She dished up a piece of chocolate cake and began to eat it, closing her eyes and savoring it.

So we were gearing up for battle. I didn't have any appetite left. My stomach was filled with tension.

Cerridwen looked at me and said, "Eat. You will need your strength. Once the battle begins everyone will be too busy to do so. You included. I'm sure the healers will need all the help they can get. It's time you used your magic for something other than defense."

"What do you mean?" I asked.

"Today you will begin to learn how to stabilize the wounded."

"Who will have time to teach me?" I imagined the Healers' space as complete chaos during a battle.

"I will *take* the time to teach you. You will assist me."

I looked at her with shock and gulped down my soup, then grabbed two chocolate chip cookies.

Olwen and Cerridwen finished and we left. The dining room stood nearly empty. It hadn't taken Cerridwen's gift for most people to figure out what was going on.

At the Healers' there was a great deal of bustling around, Lucifer was there when we arrived. As he left he came to me and said, "Take care of yourself and stay here. Remember that you are still among the living. This is the safest place. Sleep on the floor if you have to. Have someone else get you food. Do not leave this room until the battle is over and I return."

"What if you don't return?"

"Thanks for that. If I don't return there is no safe place for you here and someone will try to get you home. Now, I must go, things to do, places to be." With that he slipped through the doorway.

Cerridwen brought me to one of the beds where a young man lay. He looked particularly gray. She helped me ground myself and then focus on picking up energy from the room and moving it into the man's body. I was able to connect up with her energy and see what she was doing. We got enough energy flowing through him that I could hold it and keep it within him, while she extracted poison from the wound. A poison arrow. I watched as she used her energy to push the poison out of his body and onto a cotton cloth. Then when it was completely gone, she was able to reconnect some of the injured muscles and skin, so that the only evidence something had happened was a pinkish area where the arrow had gone in.

The man opened his eyes and looked at her, trying to speak. She gave him a few sips of water and said, "Sleep," as she waved her hand across his face. He closed his eyes and slept.

"We are finished with him," she said. We left his bed and moved to the center of the room. I copied her and ran my hands through the cone of golden light which vibrated there. "This will clean our hands of his energy, so we can go to the next patient."

I felt the energy drain off of me, then more flowed back into me. The cone turned orangish for a second, then gold again.

Her work as a healer looked seamless and easy, but I watched as she did incredibly difficult things. Mending bones and organs. I simply tried to keep the patient's energy from leaking out.

At one point the double doors opened and there was a huge influx of people carrying or dragging others. Other people and creatures came limping in, staggering and barely able to make it.

Some of them were repaired and went right back out to continue fighting. Others would be in bed for a while.

I followed Cerridwen around and did what she told me until I was so fried I couldn't stand up, let alone keep my eyes open. At which point, she pushed me towards a couch, handed me a blanket and pillow and said, sleep.

"But what will you do?"

"What I must. Now don't argue with me. Sleep, so you can get up and help again."

I staggered to the couch, lay down and don't remember anything else.

I woke to Nuada calling my name. He stood bent over me and said, "Angelica, I don't have much time to talk right now. I just wanted to let you know that Chris is conscious." Then he turned and walked off back into the fray.

I sat upright, hoping this wasn't a dream. Trying to get up my legs got tangled in the blanket and I nearly fell. Finally, I got all unwrapped and threw the blanket into a pile on the couch.

I squeezed through the crowded room and found Chris' bed.

He was sitting up, talking to a healer I didn't recognize. She looked relieved that I was there. "I need to go help the wounded. Would you please sit with him and get him oriented to the time, what's happening and his situation?"

I nodded and she left.

"What the hell does that mean? My situation?" Chris asked, his voice rising as his throat tightened.

I offered him some water and he knocked the glass from my hand and it shattered. An assistant walked by and with a wave of her hand magically swooshed the pieces into a garbage can.

All the anger and guilt which I'd put on myself for the accident, all the sadness about him losing his leg roiled up from inside me. I let him have it. "Listen, you're not twelve anymore. We're all busy here. There's a battle going on and this whole place is chaos. Lots of patients need help. I realize you're pissed off at me for killing you. So just shoot me and be done with it. I'm so tired of feeling guilty, which is pretty much all I've been doing for two years. Killing me would solve all my problems. Shall I go find you a gun?"

I felt astonished I'd blown up like that. I hadn't realized the tension had gotten to me so much.

Chris just sat there staring at me. Speechless. Finally, he said, "I'm sorry. I don't understand where I am or what I'm doing here."

"Didn't the healer try to tell you?"

"Yeah, I guess she did."

"Are you ready to listen?"

"Yeah. Are you my little sister?" he laughed.

"Not any more. I'm the same age you were when you died. So now, I guess I'm just your sister."

"Where am I?"

"Hell. This is Lucifer's home, although he calls it his lair, I think. He likes alliteration."

"If this is Hell, what are you doing here?"

"It's a really long story," I said.

He pointed to the restraints on his bed, wrapped around his knees and hips. "I don't think I'm going anywhere."

So, I spent a few minutes catching him up on my life, as well as Mom and Dad.

"Dad's acting like a prick," he said.

"I agree. That doesn't make it any less hurtful though."

"Okay, so how did I get here? The last I remember, I was walking through a mountain pass, going with some people who were running away from Hades."

"They brought you in with the refugees. They were ambushed, several people were badly injured. You were one of them."

"Is that why I can't feel my right foot?"

"Exactly." I really didn't want to be the one to have to tell him. "You can't feel it because your leg is gone below the knee."

His eyebrows rose. He didn't believe me. "Unbuckle these, please."

It took me a while, but I finally got both the restraints off his bed. He pulled the covers off and looked at his leg, moving it. The stump was bandaged and he moved it as if it hurt.

He lay his leg back down and pulled the covers back over it without a word, but his face drooped. I knew his athletic dreams had died when he did, but now this.

"Chris..."

"Can you leave me alone for a while?"

"You sure?"

"Yeah."

"Okay, I'm sure they've got work for me." I felt worse than I did before. As if it was my fault all over again. If I hadn't killed him, he wouldn't be spending eternity with half a leg.

I wandered out into the makeshift hallway between beds and over to the desk. The woman at the desk pointed me to a room I'd never noticed before. I made my way there and inside I found food and drinks.

I got a cup of coffee and a cinnamon roll, hoping to wake up fully. As I sat down to eat, Cerridwen arrived and got food as well. The roll was too dry and stuck in my mouth.

"You look like you've lost your last friend," she said.

"My brother's awake. He hates me. And he should. First I killed him and now he's lost half his leg."

"He doesn't hate you, he's just angry. You'll see."

I didn't really believe her. I just drank my coffee and ate my cinnamon roll. Sugar and caffeine.

It occurred to me that at least I wasn't out on the battlefield. What were they eating? Did they have time to eat?

"Have you heard how the battle's going?" I asked.

Cerridwen shrugged. "I've been too busy to ask."

"You were working the entire time I slept?"

"Yes."

"Aren't you tired?"

"Yes," she said. "Although I am a Goddess. I can last longer than humans, but I do need to rest occasionally. Healing drains energy even from deities."

Nuada wandered in and got food and sat with us. He looked tired as well.

"How long has the battle been going on?"

"Twenty six hours," said Cerridwen.

"Have you heard how things are going?" I asked Nuada.

"No," he said, fidgeting and looking uncomfortable.

"Aren't either of you curious?"

"We've both been through a lot of battles, so no," said Cerridwen.

"There's nothing we can do to affect the battle. All we can do is care for the wounded, perhaps sending some of them back out to fight again," said Nuada. He looked defeated.

"This is all so pointless," I said.

"War generally is," said Cerridwen.

"Pathetic and pointless. Started by gods who can't work things out in a reasonable way," said Nuada. He was clenching his coffee cup so tight I was afraid it would break.

"Who started the war?" I asked.

"Hades and Pluto. Perhaps Zeus has always been behind it, who knows?" said Cerridwen.

"Against Lucifer?" I asked.

"No, against Hecate," said Nuada. "She's the real power here. Always has been."

"Why did they start it?"

"Jealousy. They want her power, which they can never have," said Cerridwen.

"Then how can the war ever end?"

"It will only end when one side is well and truly defeated and has no more resources to wage the war."

"So, basically never?" I asked.

"This was has been going on for two thousand years. Although I think Zeus is probably the reason it's carried on so long. Hades, Pluto and Arawn would have gotten bored by now," said Cerridwen.

"Someone should turn Zeus into a dog. Or perhaps a lizard," I said.

Laughter came from the doorway. I saw Hecate standing there, laughing. She wore full body armor and held a helmet in her hand. A sword was sheathed at her side. "I'd like to see that," she said. "Please arrange it."

"Angelica's been wondering how the battle is going," said Cerridwen.

"Well, we rescued another group of refugees and scattered Pluto's forces. Hades is still holed up, but we're working on that. There was no sign of Zeus. The fabulous news is that Arawn has defected. He's joined our side. Lucifer's having a long talk with him, trying to get information out of him."

"That's terrific," said Nuada. "Now, the rest of the Celtic deities will come as well. That's more movement than we've had in eons."

"I'm hoping it will help. We're all tired of this foolish war," said Hecate. She guzzled a cup of steaming hot coffee and said, "I'm off again."

Cerridwen stood and said, "I'd better get back."

Nuada followed, so I thought I'd better go as well. I followed Cerridwen to the desk and she was directed to one of the newly occupied beds. We passed Olwen on the way and Cerridwen said something to Olwen which I didn't hear. Olwen nodded and went on her way.

The next several hours were a blur. Patient after patient. Some of whom, after we finished with them, stood up and walked back into the battle. It was truly astonishing. Many of them did not. At one point I asked her if we'd run out of beds or space for the wounded. She said no.

Hours later, she told me to go back to the room and sleep again. I went to look for Chris. His bed was occupied by someone new. The man at the desk said Chris had been released and gone to his own room. I was shocked and wondered how he would have gotten there. I hadn't seen any wheelchairs since I'd arrived here. Or crutches. Not that I'd been looking.

Chris obviously hadn't called for me, which made me feel sad. I didn't know if he'd ever forgive me for killing him. Now, he'd lost a leg and that felt like my fault as well. I was sure he'd see it that way. It made me feel like I'd lost my brother all over again. My eyes began to fill with tears, but I took a deep breath and stuffed all the pain away. I didn't want to fall apart where everyone could watch and I also felt pathetic. People were dying here. My life was a piece of cake in comparison.

I walked by the dining room, grabbed a sandwich and ate it before I fell on the couch and was out.

I woke, ate and worked with the healers. The hours stretched into days. I didn't see Chris, Olwen, Lucifer, Scathach or Hecate. Just Cerridwen, the other healers and endless patients coming through. After a week of this, the battle was declared over.

Cerridwen said, "You've done extremely well this last week. I hadn't thought you would be so skillful. You should be proud of yourself."

I realized that I was. I'd helped heal so many people and it made me feel good. I felt worth something. I nodded to her.

"Good, now go eat and sleep and look up Scathach to do some training. Don't come back here for two days at least!"

So I took one entire day off. Ate, slept, watched HellTV, ate more, slept more.

The next day after a light breakfast I went looking for Scathach at the training grounds. She and some red haired, bearded guy were going at it with swords and shields. He was bigger and stronger, but she was beating the pants off him. I took a seat in the bleachers to watch.

She was so wily. I realized what she was doing. Eons of training warriors had enhanced her ability to see clearly. It didn't take her long to figure out an opponent's weak spots. And everyone had them. Then she zeroed in on that and with her speed and skill, she wiped them out. This guy was tremendously powerful; he had a sort of red aura around him which made me think he might be a God.

Lucifer walked in the door, saw the sparring and then me. He came and sat next to me.

"How have you been?" he asked.

"Busy."

"At the Healers'?"

"Yeah."

"Well, at least you're staying out of trouble! What do you think?" he asked, pointing at the Scathach and her opponent.

"I think the guy's getting creamed."

"She's amazing isn't she? He's one of the best warriors in the world. But she's better."

"Who is he?"

"Arawn."

# CHAPTER SEVENTEEN

"THAT'S ARAWN? He's one of the Underworld and War Gods, right?"

Lucifer nodded.

"So, he's not our enemy anymore?"

"No. He changed sides. Tired of the nonsense that Zeus is handing out," said Lucifer

"So does that mean the war is almost won?"

"No, it won't be over until Zeus surrenders or is incapacitated."

"Incapacitated. That's a strange way to put it. What does that mean?" I asked.

"He needs to be incapable of harming another creature. Or being a threat to anyone."

"Is that possible?" I asked.

"Oh yes. Definitely yes. Tricky though," he said, winking at me.

"So you've got a plan for this?"

He said, "Yes, I think I have."

"Care to enlighten me about it?" I asked.

"I think I'm going to keep it to myself. If I tell anyone too soon there are too many variables that could be affected."

"So Hecate knows you've got a plan?" I was sort of wondering out loud.

"She knows I'm scheming about it, but not what the plan entails. Like I said, too many variables."

He was maddening. Now I was dying to know. But if he wasn't telling Hecate, then there was no way he'd tell me.

"How is your brother?" he asked.

"Don't know. He checked out of the Healers'. Has a room of his own. Last time I saw him he was mad at me and I think he hates the world." And probably me, I thought. That left a huge lump in my stomach.

"Understandable reaction to losing a crucial body part. I've seen him with Olwen--they have that in common at least. I think she's helping him heal."

"Is she a healer, too? I can't quite get a grasp of what she is."

"My dear, she's the Celtic Goddess of Love and Rebirth. If anyone can heal his heart, then she can."

"How could I not have seen that?" I'd never gotten around to looking her up on the computer.

"When you first met her, she was much diminished from her injury. Most people's minds store their first impressions of others."

I sat and watched the sparring for a while. Arawn almost had Scathach cornered, but she ducked out of it at the last minute, tripped him, threw him on his back and stuck her sword at his throat. He held up his hands and she took her sword away. He got up, laughing. Then they started again.

"When was the last time you were dizzy?" asked Lucifer.

I thought and I couldn't remember. "I don't know. I've been so busy working at the Healers' that I honestly don't remember. I'm getting better, aren't I?" I felt worried, not sure if I wanted to get well.

"It's not like an illness, even though we call it 'infected'. You don't get better, you just learn to control it."

"But once I do that I'll have to leave won't I?"

"Don't you want to leave?"

"This place is more like home than any place has been in the last couple of years."

"Don't you miss your friends."

"I don't have any friends." I felt my emotions close down at that, put the lid on it. I didn't want to go there.

"You just moved to a new house and a new school. The possibilities would have been endless for you to make friends."

"Yeah, all that has changed, but I'm still the same me."

"Are you sure about that?" he asked.

"Okay, so I'm a little different, but I'll never be popular. Back in the real world I'd still be that strange loner girl."

"If that's who you want to be, then you will. But it's been my experience that humans have a vast capacity for change. Especially in their early years. You're very smart and observant. If you want to be someone else, you could be. It would be your choice," he said.

"You never answered my question though. Once I learn to control the magic, do I have to leave?" I asked, again.

"No. I could never force you to leave. I'm just not sure that this is the healthiest place for you," he said.

"What does that mean?"

"Well, everyone here is either dead, a deity or an immortal creature. I'm told you've potential to become a very skilled healer. You might find a partner here, perhaps even an eternal partner, but you will not be able to have a child. And you certainly won't lead a normal life. If you should find a partner, you will age and they won't. You will die and it's a fairly large transition to go from alive to dead. Your relationship might not survive it," he said.

"I can't even picture having a romantic relationship. Who would want me?"

He stared at me with fake amazement, or maybe not fake, then asked, "Shall I stop beating them off with sticks and declare open season on you for a week? You'd be trampled."

"I don't understand," I said.

"The only reason suitors aren't lined up outside your door, well, besides the fact that you're hardly ever in your room, is that I've told everyone to leave you alone. You've had enough to deal with learning how to use the magic, so it doesn't use you. I've had countless inquiries about you, as have Hecate and Cerridwen. We've told everyone that you're off limits. Many of them have less than honorable intentions, but there's been some nice guys too."

"You haven't told me about any of this before," I said.

"It hasn't come up. We always have quite a lot to talk about, you and I. And I've been trying to protect you," he said.

"Protect me from who?"

"From everything and everyone that could do you irreparable damage." He sighed dramatically. "It's a full time job. One of many."

He was getting vague on me again. Scathach and Arawn had finished and were coming over to talk to us.

Lucifer introduced me to Arawn.

"I was wondering who this charming lady was. I was trying to impress you, but Scathach wouldn't have it. She is just too good." He bowed at me.

Lucifer raised an eyebrow at me as if to say, 'See, I told you so'.

I glared at him.

Scathach looked at me and said, "We haven't worked in a week. I suppose you didn't have time to practice, did you?"

"No, I spent all my waking hours at the Healers'."

"Well, then I'll go easy on you. And you'll need a hot bath with salts afterward."

I nodded and went to get my padded vest and a wooden sword, hoping that Lucifer and Arawn would leave.

They didn't, but I did my best to ignore them. Whenever I couldn't, Scathach reminded me to focus, painfully. Once I had the requisite number of bruises, which felt like it took ten hours, we quit for the day. I had a really nice bruise on my eyebrow which throbbed painfully.

As we were putting things away, I asked her, "How can you just have fought a battle, for seven days, and still be able to do this?"

"This is my life. You learn how to pace yourself during a battle. Some. And I rested yesterday. Also, you must realize, I am immortal, not human."

I shook my head. Her life was unimaginable to me.

As I was leaving, Lucifer and Arawn joined me.

"Care for some dinner?" asked Arawn.

"Uh, no. I'm headed for a hot bath like Scathach advised me."

"Would you like some company?" he asked.

"No, I really like to bathe alone."

"Perhaps, we could dine together later."

He was really making me nervous. I wasn't even attracted to him. Lucifer was silent, but I could almost swear he was laughing.

We were at my door. "Bye," I said closing it.

Inside, I ran a hot bath and threw in some of Scathach's bath salts, undressed and eased myself into the water. I was sore already and it wasn't even the next day. Tomorrow, I'd be in real pain. Then I'd get to do it all again.

The next morning I dressed, ate and went back to the Healers'. Nuada saw me when I entered and said, "I'd like you to work with me today."

"Where's Cerridwen?" I asked, my shoulders tightened. What was this about?

"She gave the other healers a break and now that they're back, she's taking one."

I nodded and followed him. The room held half the occupants that it did during the middle of the battle, which meant it was still crowded and nearly every bed full. These were the serious injuries. The minor ones had all been healed and the recipients walked away.

We worked on a man who had a sword run through some of his vital organs. I couldn't tell which ones. I held the space and kept the energy level, while Nuada went further in and carefully knit the organs together using his own energy.

I didn't understand how it worked. It made no sense compared to Western medicine. Then again most of these people were dead and clearly their bodies operated by different rules. It was fascinating to watch him work, I yearned to learn more from him and Cerridwen. It felt wonderful to be able to do something to help, even something which was as simple as holding the energy level stable.

Nuada said, "It's about rearranging cells and tissue at an energetic level. We are physically moving things around in their bodies. You are keeping their physical bodies from stressing out and panicking while I reconnect arteries and capillaries and knit cells back together."

I didn't want to point out that dead people shouldn't have physical bodies, because they do. They are solid, you can touch them. They wear clothes, well most of them. They feel pain and get injured and panic and laugh and eat and sleep. Clearly they can lose limbs and even die permanently. I was still trying to work out what being dead meant. It was completely different from what I'd believed my whole life.

It felt wonderful working with and sharing energy with Nuada. He was kind and gentle, but strong. And I have to admit, gorgeous, sexy and hard to stop staring at. Every time he touched me I felt tingles run through my entire body. I knew he liked me, but I doubted it was anything serious. More of a friendly acquaintance thing with him. I mean he's a God, who's lived hundreds of years. He couldn't fall for me.

At the end of our day, I ate lunch, or maybe dinner, and went to find Scathach. The training grounds were empty, but inside the weapons room there was a whole lot of yelling.

"You can't do that. She couldn't possible defend herself," said Scathach.

"She won't have to," said Lucifer. "She'll be well protected."

"She's the perfect person. He'd fall for her like a starving wolf for an injured deer," said a heavily accented voice. It sounded sort of like Arawn.

"No. It's too dangerous for her."

"I'm not sure we have a choice, if we want this war to end," said Lucifer.

"Have you run this by Hecate?" Scathach asked.

"No, she'd never agree without your consent," said Lucifer.

"With good reason. You can't use the girl as bait," she said.

"Scathach, someone has to do it. None of the rest of us are pretty enough," said Arawn.

"Have you told Angelica about this plan?" asked Scathach.

"Not yet. I wanted to talk to you first," said Lucifer.

"I don't agree, but if Hecate and Angelica and Cerridwen agree, I'll defer."

"Good," said Lucifer.

I walked into the room. "Agree to what?" I asked.

Scathach jumped in surprise. Lucifer and Arawn almost did. I felt proud I had actually surprised Scathach at something.

"How long have you been listening?" asked Lucifer, his hands on his hips.

"A little while," I said.

"Well, this is a little complicated, and clearly not the place to talk about it if eaves droppers can sneak up on us," he said.

"I'd have to agree," said Arawn.

"Let's meet in an hour in the war room. I'll have Hecate, Selene, Eren and Cerridwen meet us there. Then I'll fill you in on my idea," said Lucifer to me.

I nodded.

Lucifer and Arawn left. Scathach cleaned her sword, saying nothing for a long time. I was used to her silences, so I just stood there, waiting.

Finally, she said, "I'm going to tell you this, even though I know you haven't heard his idea yet. I'll leave it to Lucifer to explain fully. I don't like using you as bait. You are far too precious. You are alive and filled with so much magic that none of us has any idea what you're capable of. If something went wrong, if you fell into Zeus' hands I have far too many ideas about what would happen to you, none of them good. He is worse than an animal and holds nothing dear, except his own skin." She looked at me. "So before you agree to go along with this, I want you to be very sure what you might have to give up."

I nodded. I knew she meant I could die, or perhaps worse, become Zeus' pawn.

She said, "Why don't you do some stretching exercises while I shower and dress? You must be stiff."

I went out into the training ground and did a few stretches. Her shower must have taken all of two minutes, because I hadn't even made it through the whole circuit by the time she was dressed and ready to go. She wore black Capri leggings and a black tank. Except for her footwear, sandals, she would have looked right in place in any Zumba class. But not as a participant, as a teacher. No one could mistake all those ripped muscles for anything other than a perfectly toned body. Come to think of it, maybe she looked more like a body builder.

We stopped in a dining room and picked up some chocolate cake to bring to the meeting.

With her, I didn't even have to ask for directions to get to the war room. When we got there, everyone was already there, including Nuada.

# CHAPTER EIGHTEEN

I SAT NERVOUSLY on the couch, cradling my piece of cake on my knees. I'd finished it before everyone else had sat down and Lucifer started talking, while pouring coffee for everyone.

"I have an idea," he said. "It's not fully formed, because I wanted everyone's input before I developed it further."

As he paused everyone nodded. Nuada looked angry, as did Hecate and Selene. Cerridwen was serene and unreadable. Arawn looked eager. Scathach sat next to me, her face turned away, but her body tense.

He continued, "We've all agreed that Zeus is the main problem. Without him Hades and Pluto will capitulate. In order to deal with Zeus we've got to capture him and put him in a situation where he can't hurt anyone ever again. As far as we know he can't be killed."

Again everyone nodded.

"Well," said Lucifer. "We know one of his weak points is women. Young women. Beautiful young mortals. My plan is very simple. We call a truce and ask to negotiate, but with Zeus only. He must be there or negotiations will not take place."

"He won't come," said Hecate. "And do we really want to be known as truce-breakers?

"Yes, he will," said Lucifer. "We'll offer him Angelica as a gift, even if we can't agree on anything at the negotiations. I don't bloody well care if I'm known as a truce-breaker if we can end this war."

"No," said Nuada. "You can't offer up Angelica to that animal."

"Hear me out."

Nuada leaned back in his chair, arms folded.

"So, he comes to the negotiations. It's just him and Hecate and Angelica. While he's checking out Angelica, who will have spent some time with Olwen, learning to use her magic in quite another way, Hecate will turn him into a nonpoisonous snake, or a hound. He'll be under her control until we can dispose of him in the manner that befits a God given to temper tantrums."

Hecate looked thoughtful. Selene was quiet. Cerridwen was still unreadable. Lucifer's idea was fascinating. Was it possible I could do something to end this stupid war?

Nuada said, "It's too dangerous. Should anything go wrong, we'll lose Angelica. She won't survive what Zeus will do to her."

Scathach said, "There's so much that can go wrong. He'll bring others, who'll overpower Hecate and Angelica. There could be an attack. He may bring hidden weapons and kill Angelica. He could send a minotaur instead. There are so many other possibilities which could turn out badly that I can't even list them."

Cerridwen asked Hecate, "If you had him, could you turn him into something you could imprison and control?"

"Yes, I have that power. I would need help disposing of him though. I cannot think of something which would be permanent, a place to imprison him forever."

"I have a place," said Lucifer.

"Where?" asked Nuada.

"I will not speak of it. The fewer who know the less likely he is ever to be found again."

"I still do not think it is safe for Angelica," said Scathach.

"There is risk involved," acknowledge Lucifer.

"Too much risk," said Nuada.

"Selene, do you have an opinion?" asked Lucifer.

"I don't know. It would depend a great deal on where the truce was being negotiated. You know Zeus will be very particular about that. It will depend on how defensible it is. We must be able to completely hide whoever and whatever is defending Angelica. And be able to foresee any crimp Zeus would put in our plans."

Lucifer turned to me, "Angelica?"

"I don't really understand what my job would be."

"You must simply be your charming self and Olwen will help you learn to channel some of your excess magic to use as a subtle seduction. You must simply keep Zeus' mind occupied for a few minutes. Not a difficult thing to do. He's a being of voracious sexual appetite, as you may have heard. No worse than the average teenage human male. He's simply not afraid to do anything about it."

"I've never been able to get or keep any guy's attention," I said.

"You underestimate yourself my dear," said Arawn.

"I've told her that," said Lucifer, "but of course, as usual, she doesn't believe me."

"Arawn, you haven't weighed in on this," said Cerridwen. "You've spent the most time recently with Zeus, of any of us."

"He's definitely a little more unhinged than he used to be. He's never been good at sharing power, but it's getting worse. I think the most difficult part of your plan would be to get him somewhere alone. He doesn't trust either Hades or Pluto, but he certainly doesn't trust anyone in this room either. The place we choose would have to be done with great care and we should have several other possibilities in mind."

"Of course, you don't know Angelica enough to worry about her safety," said Nuada. "She holds enormous power. She is one of the reasons why so many warriors were put back on their feet during the last battle. Her potential to become a healer is prodigious."

I was astonished to hear him say that. Lucifer hinted at it and Cerridwen told me I should be proud of the help I'd given, but I thought I was spending my time with the healers because it was safe and because they desperately needed help. I had no idea Nuada felt that way.

I sat back on the couch. I'm sure my mouth was open wide enough to catch flies.

Lucifer said, "So, can we at least agree it's an interesting idea and one to pursue further?"

"What do you mean pursue further?" asked Scathach.

"I mean have Angelica spend some time working with Olwen. The rest of us spend time coming up with suitable locations. And defensive strategies. We don't know how soon he'll attack again, but we should time this to happen after his next attack. He'll think he's weakened us."

Hecate said, "I'm willing to explore the idea, but we won't be taking any action until everyone in this room agrees it's the right thing to do."

Cerridwen said, "I think Angelica should ask Olwen for a few lessons in glamour by telling her it's for her personal use. That she wants to attract someone she knows, let's say it's Nuada. I trust Olwen, but I don't think it wise for any hint of our plan to leave this room."

"I agree with that," said Lucifer. "The more people who know about it, the larger our chance for failure."

Scathach nodded her head, looking relieved. Nuada still didn't look happy about the whole thing, but grudgingly gave his consent.

I'd heard enough to make a decision. "I want to do this. If I can do anything to end this war, if all of you think this plan will work, I want to do it."

The meeting broke up and I felt antsy. I didn't know what else to do, so I went to the training ground and ran a few laps until I was tired. Then a shower and bed.

The next few days went back to normal, if there was a normal. The Healers' after breakfast, where I worked with either Cerridwen or Nuada. Then, I collected bruises from Scathach, although most days I was getting fewer than I had at the beginning. After a shower and dinner, I'd hang out with Olwen, who I persuaded to help me out with a few lessons on attracting men.

We sat in a lounge area, by the fire and she tried to teach me 'glamour' as she called it.

"It's really about accentuating what you've already got," she said. "You have lovely brown, silky hair. So you put forth the intent of making your hair so silky that your target cannot resist touching it. You have deep, blue eyes, so make them his favorite shade of blue, so that when he's near you, he needs to spend his time gazing into your eyes unable to look away at, let's say, your unattractive clothing or dirty fingernails."

"But how do I know what he likes?" I asked.

"Well, if you don't have an opportunity to study him, then you need to ramp up your efforts so that he thinks your blue eyes are the most beautiful color he's ever seen. It's all a matter of degree. Glamour can be the subtlest of all forms of magic."

"So how do you accomplish it?"

"Watch," she said.

I watched and tried to figure out what she was doing. But I found myself irresistibly drawn to her mouth. I sat and waited for her to say something with her lovely, musical voice.

"Okay, now what did I do?"

When she spoke, a form of release came with it. I said, "I don't know, I was just waiting for you to speak again."

"I was drawing your attention to my lips and voice. Away from the fact that I'm missing an arm."

I sat back in the chair, understanding. "But I'm still not clear how to get my magic to do that."

She touched my hand and it felt as if a connection was forged between the two of us. I could see her drawing some of my magic from the core of my body, where it tended to hover, and up into my eyes, filling them with magic. "That's the essence of it. Now you need to put your intent behind it."

I said to myself, '*you have the most irresistible eyes, once someone looks in them, they cannot look away*'. I felt my eyes turn almost warm.

Olwen finally jerked her attention away from me. "Okay," she said, still not looking at me, "now reverse that and turn the magic off."

I imagined the magic draining back into my core and everything returning to normal.

Finally, she looked at me and said, "That was wonderful. Overkill, but wonderful. You have very powerful magic inside you. You'll need to practice subtlety, but that was a fabulous first attempt. I had a difficult time pulling myself away. I'm a Goddess, so I could do it. I'm not sure who you're trying to attract, but I don't think he'll be able to resist you."

"That's it? That's all I have to do, is refine it?"

"That's the essence of it. The hard part is finding the right degree of strength to do what you need. If it's too strong, anyone with any awareness will be able to tell what you're doing and shake it off, like I did. You don't want him to know you're doing this. It sort of spoils the effect and will generally just piss them off. Glamour is a form of lying."

So, I spent my spare time looking in the mirror and practicing. Not that I had a lot of time. On the rare occasions when Nuada and I were alone and not working I practiced on him, trying hard to be subtle. When I failed he'd look at me with annoyance and say, "Stop it."

I didn't dare practice around Arawn or Lucifer. Or men who were strangers. So Nuada was the only one I could experiment on.

Olwen was spending some of her extra time each day with Chris. She said, "It's not that he doesn't want to see you, it's more that he's wallowing in self pity and trying to figure out what's possible for him now. He's trying to deal with his own problems and you don't really enter into it for him. Be patient, once he understands who he is again, he'll contact you."

He'd been given a fake leg to wear and sometimes he would, but mostly he used crutches. He was deep in rebellion, something he'd never done while he lived, whereas I hadn't done much other than rebel.

The days stretched on. We had rumors of attacks which never happened. A wave of major deities defected to us and was assimilated. Then several groups of refugees came to us. They were all warriors and Lucifer turned them away. He said Zeus and Hades were trying to infiltrate us, do the Trojan Horse thing and he wasn't foolish enough to fall for that. There were rumors that Lucifer was using Morrigan as a weapon. One look from her was enough to send the enemy into madness and terror. I tried not to listen to those rumors, I couldn't even think about her without feeling my blood turn to ice.

We had several meetings in the war room, arguing over places to meet with Zeus. Lucifer was working hard to break everyone down to accepting his idea.

At one point, Nuada said, "You can tell Angelica to stop using glamour on me. She's got it figured out."

"Having problems resisting her, are you?" asked Arawn, laughing. "Can't blame you. I'm glad she hasn't been practicing on me. I couldn't have taken it."

"But is she subtle enough for Zeus?" asked Lucifer.

"Yes," said Nuada, "even when I know what she's up to, I can't figure out exactly what it is she's doing, until she tells me."

"Okay," said Lucifer. "Now my latest idea is to meet someplace on Earth. Where we may encounter a few humans, but not many. Let's say in the desert. In southwest America."

"Why there?" asked Hecate.

"If it were some place like Canyonlands or Arches, the rock formations would hide a great many warriors, should we need back up. I'm partial to the Fiery Furnace in Arches," said Lucifer.

Hecate rolled her eyes.

"You could meet wearing human clothes, just you and Angelica and Zeus. There are tours twice a day, but the rest of the day hikers may come and go. It's filled with crevices and other lovely places to hide."

"Which means he'd have places to hide his people there as well," said Selene.

"We'll be there first, days ahead of time," said Lucifer. "I can send demons who love the heat and they can hold places for us and watch where his people hide."

Cerridwen said, "But don't you think he'll already have figured that out and have people there before your people?"

"Perhaps," said Lucifer. "We must not announce the meeting place too early. And we must have our people in place before we even agree on a spot."

"If you're going to offer several options, you'll need to plant many demons, several for each spot you're offering," said Scathach.

"Yes," said Lucifer.

"I think it's a good choice," said Hecate. "The first viable one we've come up with at least. We'll need to have at least two other choices."

The meeting ended with no other movement.

The next day Zeus attacked.

# CHAPTER NINETEEN

I WAS at the training grounds when we heard screeching. Gray, blue smoke wafted in through the open door. I stood and stared, terror filled my mind. The screaming made my skin crawl, I felt as if there was no hope we could win.

Scathach slapped her hands over my ears and shoved me into the equipment room. In a cabinet she pulled out earplugs and handed them to me. I felt better once they were in my ears, but I could still hear some of the screeching. She put earplugs in her own ears and pulled out small round things from a cupboard. They looked like grenades. She set off two in the main cavern, filling it with orange smoke. The blue, gray smoke thingees shriveled and fell onto the floor.

Scathach grabbed her helmet and a real sword, as well as the bag full of the orange smoke bombs. She dragged me down the hallway, throwing an orange smoke bomb wherever we found more gray, blue screamers. By the time we made it to the Healers' my throat felt raw from the smoke, but my sanity had returned.

She mouthed, "Stay," as she threw three bombs in the Healers' room. Everyone around looked relieved when the noise stopped and hurried back to work. I joined up with Cerridwen as I watched Scathach disappear out through a door.

We worked together for hours. At one point a huge bull ran through the room, tossing people aside with its horns. Cerridwen stood in its path, stopping it with magic I couldn't even see. It collapsed, panting and died. Later, meat cutters from the kitchen came and cut it up, taking the remains away.

The stench smelled nauseating and I felt relieved when we moved away to another part of the room to work. But then the Healers' never smelled good during a battle. Sweat, dirt, blood and everything else wafted through the air. It was a large room, but the air didn't circulate that well. It felt difficult for me to ignore all that and focus on the healing.

Later the whole room shook like an earthquake was taking place. Plaster or something fell from the ceiling in spirals of dust-like stuff. But the building held. I didn't see any cracks. A number of the high powered healers fanned out close to the walls, held up their arms and began chanting. If I focused on them, I could see their power take a dome shape and push outward on the walls, ceiling and floor, reinforcing the building.

More casualties poured in after that, with rumors of Zeus' lightening bolts. Some of the hallways had collapsed with people inside them. Rescue attempts were going on and the battle outside continued.

I kept going, flagged, grabbed some coffee and a ham sandwich to keep the energy flowing. Then worked a lot longer. My whole body ached and I could hardly stay awake when Cerridwen told me to go sleep in the refreshment room.

I found a couch, pillow, blanket and collapsed.

I woke to screaming. The entire place was completely black. I wanted to run, but couldn't see, so I pathetically huddled under my blanket. Gradually, torches were lit. It became very quiet, although I could hear healers going about their work and patients moaning. I drank more coffee and stood shaking for a while before I went to find Cerridwen. She was still working, but looked so weary. The other healers looked just as exhausted.

"How long has this battle been going on?" I asked her.

"We're coming into the third day," she said.

"So that's why I'm so hungry and tired."

She nodded and pointed for me to dive in and help. I took the place of the young healer she'd been working with. A look of relief swept over his face as he left.

We kept on moving from patient to patient for hours. I saw Nuada and Olwen a couple of times. After while a huge influx of patients made their way inside, followed by a grim looking Lucifer.

I overheard a couple of warriors talking while Cerridwen did triage, putting the patients in order of whom should be worked on first.

"Well, we won at least," said the man with the bull's head.

"There's no winning this war. It just goes on and on forever," said the green demon, holding his injured arm.

"It will end. Lucifer won't let this go on forever."

"I hope you're right, but I'm not holding out much hope," said the demon.

Cerridwen ushered them into their places in line and we went back to working on patients.

Later that day or night, I'm not sure which, we finished with the last patient. All the beds were filled and they were either stable or healing on their own. Only a couple healers, who'd already rested, stayed and the rest of us left for food and sleep.

I remember getting to my room and nothing else, except sleep.

Several days later I was in the dining room sitting alone eating when Chris came and sat across from me.

"How are you?" he asked.

"Okay," I said. I wasn't sure I wanted to talk with him. I felt hurt he'd dismissed me so easily before. With good reason I knew, but it opened that huge wound. Just like Mom and Dad, he'd judged me and found me worthless.

"I hear you've been working with the healers. Are you planning to stay here?"

"I don't think that's my decision to make. It'll depend on Lucifer."

"Why would you want to stay down here and not be alive?"

"What exactly have I got to go back to? Dad hates me and hasn't even talked to me for two years. Mom tolerates me, because, well, someone has too; I'm only sixteen and not exactly self supporting yet. I have no friends, I'm not talented at anything. No college is going to give me scholarships for anything. Which means I probably won't be going to college. Since I'd suck at customer service, I'm guessing I'd have a great career as say a janitor, or a graveyard security person. Or anything else where I could be my loner, loser, laughable self. Oh, but I forgot, I'm infected by magic now, so that makes me even more of a freak in the real world. I've got this little problem that I can never tell anyone about. Ever. So I can never have a truly committed and honest romantic relationship even if I could find another loser like me."

I stuffed bread into my mouth, but really, I felt like crying. I just didn't want to do it in public, so bread it was. I concentrated on the taste of the whole wheat and the texture of the sesame and sunflower seeds in the bread, savoring each mouthful. With some practice I felt sure I could master the whole food as comfort thing.

Chris just sat and stared at me. Finally, he said, "Dad won't talk to you?"

I shook my head and when my mouth was empty said, "He hasn't spoken to me since the accident."

"I never knew what an asshole he was," said Chris.

"He wasn't, before I killed you. He was always nice to me, even if I was a girl."

"Are you sure Mom feels like that?" he asked.

"I overheard a conversation she had last month with her best friend, Sarah. Mom didn't know I was home. 'She's sixteen, it'll only be a couple years till she's out on her own.' Her exact words."

"Wow. Your life wasn't like this when I was alive was it or was I just oblivious?"

"Some of it was. I mean at least Mom and Dad pretended to love me, but I've never had any friends. Never had any future ahead of me. When I shot you all the family stuff changed. Down here in Hell, people talk to me. Some of them even seem to like me. I'm learning some skills. I feel useful, even though I can't use any of this out in the real world."

Chris poured himself a glass of water.

"How is your leg doing?" I asked.

"I'm getting over it. I'm learning to use the prosthetic. Olwen has helped a lot. And they've found me a job working on their computer system. Everything's five to ten years old but I'm upgrading it all so it's not a complete dinosaur. I'm amazed at what has happened in the world since I died. Hades and Pluto were so backward, they didn't learn from humans. They think they're above all that. Lucifer has an open mind and wants to learn everything."

"So you're okay here?"

"Better than okay. I'm happy. Olwen and I are seeing each other. She's amazing."

I felt shocked at that. I didn't think deities and humans dated. I mean Zeus had lots of one night stands or maybe they were rapes, I don't know. But gods and goddesses having affairs with humans hadn't been covered in any mythology book I'd had to read, not that there were that many on my reading list.

"What about you?" He asked. "Are you happy here?"

"I don't know. When I haven't been working so hard and long that I can't keep my eyes open, I guess I've been worrying about whether I'll be sent home, or whether I can control the magic enough so that I'm not plagued with vertigo. I haven't really had a chance to be 'happy.' I'm in limbo. But I think I could be happy here, probably a better chance here than on earth, where I don't fit in anywhere."

Lucifer cruised into the room and saw me. He came over and sat down. "How's things?" he asked casually.

"Caught up on sleep. I was thinking of going to the training grounds today."

"Not a good idea," he said, then took a bite of a doughnut with pink and purple sprinkles.

"Why?"

"Morrigan's there. Working with Scathach."

"Oh, I'll stay away then."

"Why don't you do some training with me?" he asked.

"Training for what?"

"Using all that magic. Give yourself a few more days break from healing. Learn some new tricks," he said.

"Okay," I said. I wondered what he had in mind. He was being very circumspect. Maybe because of Chris. "When?"

"Tonight, after dinner. I've got work to do now. Looking for Selene."

"I haven't seen her for days."

" Well, I'll keep looking," he said, grabbing another doughnut. "These really are superb. I'll see you at dinner."

I nodded.

After dinner, I followed Lucifer down the hall. He wouldn't talk about what he wanted to teach me or where we were going. Just gave me a look that said, 'I'm not talking about it here.'

We ended up at the war room. He said, "I couldn't just come and tell you there was a meeting tonight. I know you trust Chris implicitly, but just like Olwen, I don't want anyone else outside this room to know we're planning something."

Everyone else soon showed up. I hadn't seen most of them since before the last battle. Lucifer started out the discussion. "We decided to time this after Zeus attacked again. So that's now. I think we should send a messenger to him, with three choices of locations, all of which I predict he'll reject. Then he'll offer one to three locations, which we'll probably reject. Then we'll offer the Fiery Furnace location and tell Zeus it's the last offer we'll make before we obliterate him."

He paused and said, "Do all of you agree so far?"

Scathach said, "I've gone there and I think it's defensible. I think we can keep Angelica as safe there as anywhere."

Hecate and Selene nodded.

Arawn said, "Yes."

Cerridwen asked, "Is Morrigan going to be there?"

# CHAPTER TWENTY

I SHUDDERED AT HER NAME.

Scathach said, "Yes, I think she'll do her part flawlessly."

"What part is that I asked?" I didn't want to be anywhere near her.

"She will be able to keep away most anyone who Zeus might ask for help," said Scathach.

"But I don't know if I can be around her without passing out."

Cerridwen unwrapped a glowing golden stone. It was the color of amber and had a hole in it, through which a silver chain was threaded. She put it around my neck and inside my shirt.

"This will help you keep a clearer head," she said. "It will help you channel your magic when you're near her."

Lucifer went to the door and said, "Morrigan, please come in."

A cold draft preceded her into the room. It took all my strength to look at her. Her long dark cloak seemed to be made of dried corpses and she glowed as if she contained the souls from thousands of people. The smell of death hung on her like mist surrounding water. I knew what death smelled like. It smelled like the Healers' when a battle was going on. Her face looked cold, blue and exotically beautiful. Her eyes were deep, dark wells of release. I felt myself drawn to them. I wanted that release so much, more than I'd ever wanted anything.

Nuada touched my arm. "Angelica, the stone."

His touch warmed me and I remembered. I pressed the stone close to my skin, closing my eyes. A warm glimmer began in my center and spread throughout my body as the magic filled me, pushing her presence farther away. Eventually, I opened my eyes and could still keep that luminescence.

Cerridwen said, "Good. You had me worried there for a second."

Nuada asked, "Do you think we can pull this off? Capture Zeus and incapacitate him and keep Angelica safe?"

"I think it's possible," Hecate said. "I don't think we'll be safe for much longer in Lucifer's fine home. During the last battle you saw how they almost cracked open the Healers' room. If they had, Angelica would most likely have been a casualty. We will have to move and hide again. I don't know that we'll find or create another place as safe as this. Since Zeus has come out of the closet as part of this war, he's ramped things up. We will have to send Angelica home before she's ready in order to keep her safe. I'm not entirely sure she'll be safe on earth either."

"What do you mean?" Nuada asked. "Surely that's the one place she will be safe, utterly unconnected with us."

"She's been here with us too long and learned too much. Become too skilled. Now she's a valuable commodity and we think her identity has been betrayed to the enemy," said Lucifer, sadly.

"Betrayed by whom," asked Nuada, his voice rising.

"Archimedes was standing by Hades in the last battle, or cringing, I should say," said Lucifer.

"The little rat," said Scathach. "I'd love to get my hands on him."

"I should have left him in the mirror," I said.

"It would have been safer," said Lucifer. He turned to me, "I don't think you will be safe on earth until Zeus has been defeated. Angelica how does this plan sound to you?"

"I'm afraid, but I want to try. If I can do anything to help end this war, it will be worth whatever happens to me. Will I be near Morrigan?"

"Probably not," she said, with a gravelly voice. "But if I need to come near you, I will not look at you. I did it now as a test. So you could try to resist me."

I'd never heard her speak and her voice sent chills through me. I nodded not looking at her, "I can do this. I'll need to go over the exact sequence of things though."

"We'll arrange that as soon as we have a confirmation that he'll meet with us. Once a location is set, we'll arrange to meet less than twenty-four hours after that. That will give him a shorter time to round up an army and get it in place," said Hecate.

Nuada agreed to the plan, but I could see he was unhappy about it.

The meeting broke up and I returned to my room. So, I wasn't safe anywhere, even at home. I felt relieved that Lucifer wouldn't send me back. I'd get to stay with everyone at least. With my new adopted family.

The next few days I worked with Hecate, Scathach and Lucifer to get things down. Zeus agreed to meet, since Lucifer begged, saying he wasn't sure he could survive another attack by Zeus. I knew he was also bulking up our defenses in case Zeus decided to spring a surprise attack on us. And I knew Lucifer was figuring out where his people could move next if this place was compromised.

The one time I popped into the Healers', Nuada cornered me and dragged me into the refreshment room.

"Listen," he said, his voice echoing in the bare room. "Zeus is incredibly powerful. And easily angered. He's like a bomb waiting to go off. I'm not happy with this plan, but I do understand that we don't have a better one. He will be attracted to you. I just want to make sure that you aren't on the wrong end of his anger."

"I'll be as safe as I can. There's only so much I can do if things go badly," I said.

"If they do, stay by Hecate or Morrigan if you can get to her. She'll protect you."

"Okay."

"Stay safe," he said.

I nodded.

There didn't seem like much else to say.

The next day I saw Chris in the dining room again. He said, "Lucifer is having me set up another computer network at another location, so I don't know when I'll see you again."

"Where?"

"I can't say. But if this place blows, they'll send you all there."

I nodded.

"Olwen's coming with me to set up the Healers' room there."

"I haven't seen her for a long time, I've been so busy."

"You won't know that she's wearing a fake arm then. She did it to prove to me that I was being pigheaded for not wearing my prosthetic. She loves it and says it conducts healing energy better than her real arm."

I smiled. I was glad he'd found someone to share his life with, his death rather. I hugged him and he left.

There was a lot going on. Scathach kept busy helping to beef up defenses for Lucifer's Lair. Lucifer coached a select team of warriors for what I knew he called the Fiery Furnace Foray. Hecate and Selene negotiated a location with Zeus. Nuada and Cerridwen were healing. I don't know what Arawn was doing, I didn't ask. I wasn't asking about Morrigan either. So I was alone with my neuroses. I should have been practicing various exercises, and I did, but mostly I was driving myself crazy.

Finally three days later, Lucifer caught me as I lurked around the training grounds, watching the really good fighters.

"Come," he said.

I followed him to the war room. Soon afterward everyone else joined us, except Morrigan.

Hecate said, "We made our proposal to Zeus with three possible meeting locations on our turf. He countered with three on his turf. Then we settled on meeting at the Fiery Furnace. Tonight, just after sunset."

I realized I was hyperventilating and began forcing myself to take slow deep breaths.

Lucifer said, "Our warriors and Morrigan were in place yesterday before we made that offer. We are all set to go." He looked at me.

I nodded. Only five hours away. I felt relieved no one had told me sooner. I'd probably have tied myself in knots.

"We are allowed to bring one person with us," said Hecate to me. "I am choosing to leave Lucifer and Scathach in charge of the defenses here. And Cerridwen will be needed by the healers."

Arawn said, "I will come."

Lucifer said, "No, I need you here. If things go wrong, I will need the most powerful warriors to hold this place till we can evacuate."

"That leaves Selene and I," said Nuada.

"I will leave Selene in charge of the people here. She will lead the evacuation," said Hecate.

"So, I'm coming because I can provide what?" Nuada asked, annoyed.

Hecate stared at him and said, "You can provide what will help the most. If I am stuck battling Zeus, you will get Angelica out of there and to safety."

Nuada looked relieved. I felt oddly relieved as well.

I ate a light meal in the war room, none of which I remember. Lucifer went over the plans with us all again and again.

Then Hecate, Selene and I went to Hecate's quarters to dress.

They messed around with my hair until it was to their liking and put me in a white, peasanty sort of dress made of thin cotton. I wore the magic stone which dropped below the neckline, between my breasts. I demanded sensible shoes, so we settled on white running shoes in case I had to. I wore a belt around my waist with a sheathed knife, my only weapon, but Selene pointed out it would be enough combined with my magic.

Hecate wore a pale blue dress, almost floor length, and bound in an x across her bodice with jewels that looked like amethyst. She wore many rings and her long hair sat piled on top of her head and held with a comb encrusted with gems as well. She carried no weapon. On her feet were silver sandals. She looked regal and powerful. I wouldn't have messed with her.

Somehow the time passed and we returned to the war room. The only person there was Nuada. Everyone else was doing their job. Selene stood still, her eyes closed and I could feel the energy radiating from her. A bubble of blue light formed in front of her, small at first, it grew to about seven feet wide and tall. Hecate, Nuada and I stepped into it.

Once inside we walked through it and out.

I gasped as the dry heat of the desert hit my lungs. It must have been around ninety degrees. The stars looked fabulously bright and a full moon hovered on the horizon. Hecate produced light from one of her pockets as did Nuada. I had no pockets. Even though the full moon was still low in the sky, the light was good.

The rock formations cast huge shadows which would make it rough going if I had to run. And where would I run to? I couldn't open the portal. Only Nuada, Selene and Hecate could. Or maybe some of the other warriors who were hidden around us. I didn't have that skill and it worried me.

The air felt dry and the breeze brushed us with a slight coolness. We walked up the path to a flat area and waited. Someone had erected Greek columns to form a circle. Except they weren't white. They were made of the reddish rock which surrounded us. Inside was a tile floor covered with designs of black snakes and hounds for Hecate and golden lightening bolts as a concession to Zeus. Attached to the columns glowed torches which eerily lit everything.

It didn't take long for Zeus to arrive with his delegation. I couldn't see at first who he brought with him.

Then I saw a huge form in the dark. Two massive, scaly legs which turned out to be snakes. When it bent down into the torchlight, I could see the body of a man and two arms which ended in a gazillion dragon heads where hands would normally be. The head was a man's head with a long beard and white scary eyes. He also had a huge pair of scaly wings. I didn't know who or what it was, but it was taller than a lot of the rock formations surrounding us.

Hecate nodded and said, "Typhon."

"My Lady," it said, with a deep, rumbling voice. "And who have we here?"

"Angelica," I said in my most musical voice. The one Olwen had taught me.

"Nuada," he said.

"Ah. I don't know either of you," said Typhon and stood up. He seemed to blot out the stars.

Behind Typhon's legs I could see a glowing white figure. It moved between his legs towards us. As it came closer, the form materialized into a man wearing a white toga. He was tall with white hair, his face was that sort which people called ruggedly handsome. I might have thought so if I hadn't known who he was.

Zeus said, "Hecate, it is good to see you."

"Zeus, an experience, as always."

He laughed. "So you wish to talk about a treaty?"

"Right to the point, I see."

This was my cue to start my work in earnest. I sighed, as if his magnificence was too much for a mere mortal like myself. He was impressive. He carried only a short knife and a long staff. I figured the staff was the real weapon.

"All right, all right," he said. "Would you care to introduce your two companions?"

"This is Nuada, one of the Celtic deities of healing, warfare and much more," she said, pointing to him.

Zeus nodded.

"And this is Angelica, a mortal who unfortunately has been infected with magic by releasing one of ours from a mirror. Of course she doesn't know how to use it, but we're not sure if it's safe to let her return to earth, given her condition. I thought she'd made a nice gift for you. That is of course, if you'd like her."

Zeus gave me his full attention. I knew he was looking for a trap. I stood there, trying to look both shy, but fascinated by him. A difficult bridge to balance on.

He walked around me. I felt as if I was naked and every wrinkle, scratch and bruise was being scrutinized.

"She's acceptable," he said.

Which made me mad. It's not like I've ever thought of myself as a great beauty. But having this old, wrinkled, egotistical prick call me just 'acceptable' really pissed me off.

He and Hecate started into their negotiations. I didn't really pay attention to them, but put all my effort into my eyes, my lips, my soft skin, and my smooth, silky hair. Oh and the pert breasts which were nearly hanging out of my dress. And my long legs. Now and then Zeus would look at me and I'd smile. Shyly of course.

I noticed him looking at me more and more frequently as he and Hecate wrangled over territory. Nuada stood on the other side of me, lounging on his drawn sword, eyeing Typhon. Typhon was standing up straight, looking around and breathing deeply, like a prisoner freed from their prison, who's just thankful for being alive. I wondered how we'd get around him once Hecate had transformed Zeus. I didn't think even Morrigan would be any use against him. But maybe Scathach had contacted Lucifer and brought in something or someone who'd be a match for him. I wasn't sure what that could be. He was like four stories tall.

I heard owls hooing and coyotes howling. I didn't know if they were real or a signal, like in old movies. Zeus stared at my breasts. I gave a deep sigh, directing the magic to show off how creamy they looked and my nipples tightened. I knew they showed through the dress. As I looked around, I noticed Nuada had his head down, not looking at me. His eyes were open though and I felt sure he was taking in everything.

Hecate was talking about concessions she and Lucifer were willing to make and I saw her holding one of her large crystal rings and rubbing it between her hands, as if she was playing with it. I was amazed she could work magic and carry on a conversation at the same time. I focused on doing my part. All at once everything happened.

# CHAPTER TWENTY-ONE

ZEUS BEGAN TO SHRINK. He tried to cry out but Hecate had silenced him. Nuada replicated Zeus' voice, so it sounded like Zeus and Hecate still carried on the negotiations.

Finally, Zeus stood about a foot tall, Hecate pointed at him and he began to turn slender, green and scaly. His arms and legs disappeared and he slithered on the stone tiles. Hecate picked him up and slipped him into a metallic bag which she tied. I felt nauseous. This was all wrong.

Strange birdlike creatures dove at us, shrieking. They looked like huge eagles with glowing green eyes and lizard heads.

I drew my knife and summoned my magic which shot through the knife and beyond it, bringing down the bird. It hit the ground and turned back towards me, hissing.

I saw a dark shape move toward us and I knew it was Morrigan. She attacked one of the bird things, drawing it towards her.

I stood in front of Hecate, leaving her to deal with Zeus. That was the important thing, everything else paled. Once again I shot magic out the end of my knife as the bird charged at me. This blow caught it in the chest, but it kept coming.

Hecate stood behind me, chanting quietly and working on sealing in Zeus.

I knew Nuada was in charge of Typhon.

I needed to deal with the birds. I shot another blow at the one on the ground and it went down. Another one dive-bombed me. My energy weakened. I connected with the earth to pull more power.

I refocused and aimed at the third bird coming at me. I hit it. It screamed at me, just as another one flew past. A claw scraped my arm, drawing blood.

A light glimmered at the edge of the circle of columns, right between Typhon's legs and snakelike tails.

Nuada appeared beside me and yelled, "Run." He pointed at the light. I hesitated and he pushed me.

I ran for the portal, hoping Typhon wouldn't move. The smell was distinctly fishy and nauseating. It seemed to take forever.

I felt afraid my heart would explode. I wove through the columns and into the portal, finding myself in the war room, with Selene. Hecate followed shortly after.

I stood shaking, watching as the portal closed. Nuada didn't make it back.

Selene said, "It closed from the other side. Nuada, or someone else closed it."

Hecate said, "He'll be dealing with Typhon. Zeus' spell on Typhon was broken when he became a snake. Typhon is running wild.

I felt horribly worried about Nuada.

Hecate hurried out of the war room. Selene and I followed her. My arm throbbed. It weeped yellow, greenish stuff, which I knew couldn't be good, but dealing with Zeus was more important.

We went down a spiral staircase, deeper and deeper into the earth. The air got warmer and warmer. The stairway emptied into a huge cavern cut in half by a river of what looked like molten lava. The sulphur fumes smelled awful as we walked on a ledge next to the river. We passed through the cave to one filled with stalactites and stalagmites. This cave was much cooler. At the far end of it ran a river of black water. A boat was moored near the edge. A man stood in it, he looked hunched over and almost skeletal. In the dim light, I saw him gaze up at us.

"Hecate, Selene and Angelica," he said.

"Charon, will you ferry us across and then back again?" asked Hecate.

"I will take you and Selene. Angelica must wait until she's dead."

Hecate turned to me and said, "Wait here until we return. Taking care of this snake may take awhile."

I nodded and found a rock to sit on. I sat and worried about the events of the day as I watched the small boat disappear on the horizon, the protection of Hecate and Selene going with it. I pulled my knife out in case I needed it, the rock got colder and so did I, but I couldn't seem to make myself leave.

I wondered if I should go back by myself, but I didn't want to leave without being sure Hecate and Selene had accomplished whatever they were planning with Zeus. My arm hurt more than it had. I tried to run some healing energy through it, but felt tapped out.

I must have fallen asleep leaning against a larger rock, because the next thing I knew, a hand touched my shoulder, jerking me awake. I felt really cold, and realized I'd been shivering in my sleep.

A shadowy form stood above me. Lucifer.

"Angelica, what are you doing here?"

"Waiting for Hecate and Selene to return."

"Did they get him?"

"Yes, but Nuada didn't come back with us. We think he had to deal with Typhon."

"Typhon? However did Zeus manage to persuade Typhon to help him?" Lucifer asked.

"I don't know. I've never heard of him before now."

"He's the father of most of the monsters. Medusa, Cerberus, all the others. He's a volcano monster who Zeus once overpowered and trapped beneath a mountain where he's been ever since."

"Impressive since he's a really, big guy." My teeth were chattering.

"Come, let's go back up. You look like you're freezing. I just wanted to come here and check since Selene wasn't in the war room. We've done everything possible. It's all up to Hecate and Selene now."

Lucifer led me back past the lava river and up the stairs. He looked at me and asked, "Are you sure you're feeling all right?"

"I'm just so tired," I said. I didn't think I could walk another step. Somehow I did.

As we walked down the hallway to a dining room to get some food, he said, "Your arm is scratched and bleeding. How?"

"Some weird bird women attacked us."

"Weird how?" he asked.

"I didn't see them well. Large, like a bald eagle, but glowing green eyes and no feathers on their humanlike heads, sort of reptilian looking."

He looked alarmed, then covered it up with a smile and said, "The Furies. Let's go to the Healers' and see if Nuada has returned. Or Scathach or Morrigan."

I nodded. I'd love to be sure everyone was safe.

We walked for what seemed like forever. I couldn't feel my arm anymore. Finally, I walked so slowly that I stopped and fell. I felt Lucifer catch me and lift me up to carry me. That's the last I remembered.

# CHAPTER TWENTY-TWO

I WOKE to bright light with a fresco on the ceiling. I was at the Healers'. No one was sitting around me. I tried sitting up, but my body felt numb. Everything looked peculiar. There were no curtains around my bed and the Healers' was almost empty. So there hadn't been a battle or retaliation yet for kidnapping Zeus.

Eventually a dark, hooded figure came and stood next to me. "How do you feel, child?"

Cerridwen.

I tried to talk, but couldn't seem to get anything out.

"You probably can't talk yet. Sometimes the venom affects people that way."

"Venom?" I managed to croak out.

"From one of the Erinyes' talons. One of the Furies. I have to tell you that we're not sure whether you will live or not. The venom is coursing through your veins. We are using herbs to detoxify you, but we're not used to healing the living here."

I nodded and fell back into my dreams.

I dreamt of Typhon. When Zeus turned into a snake, Typhon was released from his bondage. He flew straight up in the air, rocketing like a spaceship. The heat of his departure melted the rocks on which he'd stood. In the dream I watched as every living thing in the area was charred beyond recognition. That included Scathach and Morrigan. Chris and Nuada. Lucifer was the only one unscathed.

I woke later, groggy and sweating. It took me quite a while to figure out where I was. Still at the Healers'. I didn't know if I was alive or dead. Sleeping in the chair next to my bed was Nuada. He looked peaceful, even though his face and arms were covered with scratches, gashes and bruises. He'd survived at least. I worried about everyone else. Had Hecate neutralized Zeus? Was the war over? I tried to talk, but couldn't. I waved my arms or tried to, and my fingers flapped around a little, but that was it.

It was enough. Nuada shot up from the chair, wide awake and ready to attack, then he realized the noise was just my fingers flopping on the blanket.

"You're awake," he said, smiling, even though he looked weary. He sat back down in the chair and got the glass of water off my table, bringing it to my lips and cradling my head with his other hand. I drank a little, but still couldn't speak in any understandable way.

He asked, "Can you speak yet?"

I tried, but words wouldn't come to my brain, except for hello. What came out of my mouth was so garbled, it didn't even resemble the word.

"Sometimes afterwards it takes awhile before clear thought and speech returns."

After what I wondered? I raised my hands and shrugged my shoulders. He looked puzzled. Then he left and returned with Olwen and Cerridwen.

Cerridwen looked at me and sighed. "What we all dreaded has happened. You are dead Angelica." She paused to let this sink in.

So this was what it felt like to be dead? I didn't feel any different except my brain didn't work and my body wouldn't do what I wanted it to do. I didn't know what to make of any of this. How would life be different now that I was dead? I still felt alive. I stared at her helplessly, hoping she could answer me.

Cerridwen said, "Lucifer should be here to do this. It's not my work to orient the dead and I don't really know what to say. I've never been dead." She looked at Olwen and Nuada, but I knew they'd never been dead either, being immortal.

She continued, "Lucifer has gone in search of Hecate and Selene. They haven't returned yet."

I tried sitting up, but again, my body wouldn't quite do the job. Why had Hecate and Selene not returned? Had there been a problem with Zeus? Had they been attacked? I flailed and flapped about, trying to ask questions which my vocal cords wouldn't communicate.

Then it seemed as if the entire room darkened and a cold breeze blew through it. Fear flooded my thoughts. Across the room I could see a woman with fire engine red hair dressed in a red cloak. She had a crow on her shoulder and darkness followed her across the room like a river. I couldn't see her face, it was all in shadow. Cerridwen and Olwen stepped aside to let her come closer. Nuada stayed touching my shoulder.

"Angelica, Lucifer is not here to help you, so I have come. Walk with me."

I wanted to protest that it was impossible, but with a wave of her hand, my body sat up and my legs swung around until they touched the floor. I could stand and walk. She hesitated, waiting for me. I knew, after hearing her voice, that this was Morrigan.

Heat filled me as I walked beside her and my skimpy little white dress felt warm enough. I was barefoot, but the floor was smooth and warm beneath my feet.

I tried to talk but she stopped me and said, "Your voice will return with time, you have no need of speech with me. Just open your mind and I will see your thoughts."

I took several deep breaths and tried to imagine my mind as a house with all the doors and windows open. Then I imagined the outer walls disappearing. The answers to my questions came.

She showed me the battle which had taken place after Hecate and I fled the Fiery Furnace. The Furies had attacked Nuada.

Typhon, released from Zeus' control had decided to change sides and he slapped the Furies around with his feet and wings and his dragon-mouthed hands. He finally inflicted enough damage on them that they bolted. His movements caused the earth to shake like a major earthquake. Finished with the Furies, Typhon shot into the air like a rocket, burning brightly. He circled the earth several times before coming to rest on the islands of Indonesia and triggering a volcanic eruption, which was still spewing lava.

Scathach, Nuada, the warriors and Morrigan had escaped through a portal which Morrigan opened. The land around where Typhon had stood, melted and hardened into solid rock, like lava. The fate of Zeus' warriors was unknown. I remembered my dream of Typhon flying and the melted rock he left behind. Relief spread through me that people weren't harmed like in my dream. That was my fear showing up in dream form.

I'd been out for a week. Three days ago, Lucifer had put Cerridwen in charge of the complex and taken his best warriors in search of Hecate and Selene. Scathach remained in charge of the war. Arawn had vanished. No one could find any trace of him or had any idea where he might have gone, although several theories had surfaced. Cerridwen decided to evacuate Lucifer's Lair and was in the process of moving everyone to the new location.

Morrigan welcomed me to death. She gave me love in such a way as I've never felt before. I felt complete and like I finally belonged somewhere. I no longer felt afraid of her, although I respected her astonishing power.

I realized that even though I was dead, I still needed to finish what I'd started in Hell. I needed to grow up and keep taking responsibility for my own life. I may not be able to have a child anymore, but that didn't need to stop me from growing. It would just be harder now that I was dead. We seemed to walk in endless halls which led nowhere and when we finished I found myself back at the Healers'.

Cerridwen and Olwen had left already. Morrigan disappeared, but Nuada was waiting for me. He took me to the portal.

I walked through, and felt a weird sensation as if moving through rubber cement, and I found myself in a large open room. It was filled with light and bright colors. Tall, blue columns held up the ceiling and between them were windows made of red, green and yellow stained glass in an art nouveau style. It was as if Greek Architecture mated with Medieval stained glass and then had an affair with the 1930's. The result was beautiful and breathtaking.

Out of the floor vines sprouted and grew up the columns. This room felt filled with life.

"Are we still in the Underworld?" I asked Nuada, my voice croaking, but at least I could get words out.

"Yes, this is our new home. I hope. Provided the war is over. And Hecate, Selene and Lucifer return. We made sure Arawn did not know of this place."

"You didn't trust him before?" I asked

"Some of us didn't. Enough that Lucifer kept him out of the most important parts of our plans."

"But he knew what Hecate had planned for Zeus."

"He knew what, but not where she would take him. And he didn't know where we were sending our entire population. So we have time to recover from our last strike at them."

My brain told me I was missing something. "I don't understand."

"While you were unconscious and passing from the world of the living into the land of the dead, you missed what we hope will be the last battle of the Underworld." Lucifer struck just after you, Hecate and I went to meet Zeus. Arawn did not arrive for the battle. But without Zeus' help and because their forces were so depleted, Hades and Pluto were crushed."

"So the war is over?" I asked.

"We hope so. They have surrendered. There have been no negotiations past that. I think since Zeus and his troops have failed to return that Hades and Pluto are afraid to negotiate. A treaty breaker is not to be trusted, although we knew that going into it."

I felt relieved that this awful war which had lasted far too long might actually be over. Nuada led me to a door between two of the columns. We went outside onto a large balcony. Pots of growing things sat next to the stone railing. Below lay rows of grapes, patches of wheat and fruit trees. In the distance lay the sea. People worked in the fields and boats floated on the water. In a pasture cattle grazed. We went down some steps and there sat a table laden with food.

My mouth watered. How long had it been since I ate?

We sat down. I dished up roast beef, mashed potatoes, gravy, Brussel sprouts, a dinner roll and a glass of milk. Nuada ate slowly, although not as much as I did. He was trying not to laugh at me as I inhaled the food.

I don't know how it's possible, but food tasted even better now that I was dead. Maybe it was spiced differently, maybe my body had less distractions, I don't know. But it was the best meal I'd ever had.

I finished eating and Nuada showed me around. He took my arm as he led me down a broad outdoor staircase. The entire place seemed to be terraced all the way down to the sea. This was obviously where all the food came from for Hecate's Palace and Lucifer's Lair. The rich farmland of the Underworld. The Elysian fields or the Greek version of paradise.

It did seem like paradise. The sun shone and apparently it rained for two hours every night leaving the fields watered and the streams flowing. Snow covered mountains crouched in the distance across the sea. There were glorious sunrises and sunsets. There was just enough work for everyone to be employed for four hours a day and the rest of the time people exercised and created art. And played. And fell in love. At least they had the freedom to do those things now, Nuada said, since the war was over.

He showed me my private quarters which were surprisingly spacious and airy and came with a view of the water. Then we went through the kitchens, where I grabbed a fresh chocolate chip cookie. Then to the Healers' where we found Cerridwen and Olwen making rounds and checking on the few people still there from the last battle. Then to the computer center where Chris was working to fix a bug which kept cropping up in their video surveillance of Earth, and Hades' and Pluto's people.

Hades' and Pluto's people had been moved to a place they wouldn't be able to defend in case they caused trouble. But it also had good farmland, livestock and fresh clean water. They had been denied all that for a good long time thanks to Hades' and Pluto's ambitions. Now they had the raw materials to get on with their afterlives.

Then Nuada took me to the training grounds. It was larger than the one at Lucifer's Lair. And outside in the sun. Warriors were training. Scathach stood in the middle, whacking away at some guy twice her size. And winning. It felt glorious to watch her. She moved like a panther.

The next thing I knew, Nuada was holding me up. I'd fallen asleep, standing up. He walked me back to my quarters and said, "Go to bed. Sleep as long as you possibly can. I'll check on you tomorrow."

I walked in and fell right onto the bed, sound asleep.

I woke to screaming. It was dark. I realized the screaming was my own and began shivering. I'd had a dream about Hecate and Selene.

Trapped in ice deep beneath the earth. I'd been trapped with them, struggling to breathe. It felt horrifying, gasping for breath, the chest-crushing pain of not being able to get any air. It was cold and hard. My skin had been turning blue as I tried to claw my way out.

I got up and drank some water, walked around and looked out the window at the moon shining on the sea. I opened the window to let the breeze in, the salty, seaweedy ocean air. It took about half an hour before I could relax again. I went back to sleep and slept a long time.

When I woke again it was daytime. I got up, washed my face in a basin, dressed in white pants, a turquoise tunic and sandals. Brushing my hair, which had grown a lot, I wondered how long I'd been in the Underworld. How much time had passed on earth? I wondered if Mom missed me. Probably. There was no way I could go back and explain though. I hoped she wouldn't blame herself. She tried to be a good parent. I missed her, but I'd felt that way since Chris died. She had left me then, just not as obviously as Dad did.

After dressing, I found my way back out to the balcony and sat at the table. Cerridwen was there. We ate in silence, I was starving again. I guessed from the food choice, soup and sandwich makings that it was lunchtime. Didn't know which day though or how long I had slept. Or if anything had changed.

After I'd finished, I asked Cerridwen, "Have Hecate, Selene or Lucifer come back yet?"

"Lucifer and his warriors returned late last night. Without Hecate and Selene. He is distraught," she said, shaking her head.

I felt pain in my chest and stomach. Where could they be? "Where is he?"

"In the solarium, where you first came in, at least the last time I saw him. Why?"

"I had a dream. About Hecate and Selene. And me. In a dark, cold, icy place. I don't know if it's where they went or if it was just a dream." I held up my hands in question.

She gave me a piercing look and said, "Let's find out. I don't know where they were going."

We found him in middle of the solarium, stretched out on the floor, absorbing sunlight. Seemingly asleep; he opened his eyes when we came in.

"Lucifer," said Cerridwen, "Angelica has had a dream you might want to hear."

He sighed and in one fluid movement, stood and motioned us over to a pair of stone benches. We sat and he said, "I'm sorry I was unavailable to welcome you to the Underworld, Angelica. But I'm sure Morrigan did a fine job."

"Yes, she did."

"I'm both sad that your life is gone and happy you will not be leaving us."

I nodded.

"Now, tell me your dream."

I told him the bit I could remember which was the three of us encased in ice and unable to breathe.

He looked alarmed and said, "I know where they are, but it's clear you must come with me. Go change into warm clothes and meet me back here. I will get who we need. Cerridwen, would you be so good as to get Nuada?"

"Of course, but where are you going?"

"Beneath Mt. Olympus."

"How did Charon get them there?" Cerridwen asked.

"He dropped them off just on the other side of the river. It's not where I told Hecate to go. I don't know what happened."

Lucifer looked at me and said, "Go, get ready."

I bolted towards my room. Cerridwen followed me out to find Nuada. Lucifer went in search of whoever he was bringing.

In my closet I found warm, fuzzy pants, a thick wool sweater and slip on boots. There were also some wool socks to put on and a warm, warm coat. I changed and grabbed gloves and a hat. It must get really cold around here in winter, I thought, to need all those clothes.

I returned to the solarium, carrying the coat, gloves and hat. I'd strapped on my knife, not sure if I could get to it under the coat, or if I'd have to wear it on the outside.

Nuada appeared, dressed in winter clothes as well and wearing a backpack. He looked grim. I wondered what lived under Mt. Olympus.

Finally, Lucifer entered, followed by several warriors and a huge, two-headed dragon. Well, it wasn't huge in height or width, just very, very long. A snake with legs and a fluttery finlike thing on its spine and five sets of legs. It was purple and blue and crimson, and very beautiful. The warriors didn't seem to be afraid of it but I noticed they kept well ahead of both those roving heads.

Lucifer was dressed in white fur. He wore a backpack somehow, fitted around his wings and filled with tools. I could see the handles sticking out. He opened a portal and Nuada and I followed him through. It was the same glue-like substance and I realized that the way the portals felt had changed when I died. The dragon brought up the rear, snuffling and sniffing.

We came out the other side of the portal and went down into the cave where Charon had picked up Hecate and Selene, next to the river.

Lucifer nodded at Charon and gave him gold coins. It took three boatloads to take us all across. The dragon was too large for the boat and swam swiftly next to it, clearly more at home in the water than on land. We waited silently on the far shore until everyone was across.

Then off we went into the darkness, lit by a couple of rocks the warriors carried. I'd started calling them glow stones. Lucifer walked on ahead of us, evidently he could see in the dark. His face still wearing the grim expression he'd had since Hecate disappeared.

We covered the flat plain by the river and entered into a tunnel. It was wide enough to walk upright for an hour or two, although rather creepy. Nothing seemed to live there at least. Not even mold or fungus. Then it began to get bitter cold. The tunnel climbed a little and became glacial. I put my coat, hat and gloves on. It seemed to go on forever. At one point Nuada offered me water and some dried meat. I felt grateful he at least was thinking. It hadn't occurred to me to bring food and water.

We walked and walked and walked. No one spoke, although I'm not sure why. Somehow it felt sacrilegious to be here, but I couldn't put my finger on exactly why it would be. If we were going beneath Mt. Olympus to rescue two Greek Goddesses, even though they'd imprisoned the most well-known, maybe the most powerful Greek God, what was the problem? Given, Lucifer was a Christian construct and Nuada was Celtic, the warriors were men with animal heads so that made them what, Egyptian? I was simply a dead American. Not sure what our slithery friend back there was, a Chinese dragon? Or from the U.K.? At any rate, it felt as if we shouldn't be there. As if we were getting tangled up in things that were not our business, and we were sure to get in trouble for it.

However none of us were about to stop looking for Hecate and Selene. It was clear to me that Lucifer would risk everything for Hecate.

I felt the freezing cold. My legs got so numb that I periodically stumbled and once I almost fell, but Nuada caught me, the heat of his skin temporarily warming me all the way through. We kept going forward into the darkness which seemed to last forever.

# CHAPTER TWENTY-THREE

ALL OF A SUDDEN the tunnel descended rapidly. Instead of flat floor there were small, slippery steps. I braced my hands on the wall to keep from falling on the warrior in front of me. Starting to go crazy in the dark iciness, I began counting steps. I stopped after five hundred and forty-nine. Our footfalls echoed loudly around us. My body ached from the cold and from walking. The tunnel leveled out again and opened out into a large cavern.

In the center of the cavern an eerie blue globe hung in mid air. When all the glow stones surrounded it I could see it was transparent except for a few dark spots. I couldn't tell how the globe hung there, there was no wire or connection that I could see. The ball rotated slowly. It was large, about the size of two mini-vans squished together and made into a ball.

Lucifer stared at it and began to sob. I didn't understand until the globe slowly turned and I could see Hecate's face pressed against the side. She moved slightly. Still alive, but imprisoned. The other dark shape in there must be Selene.

"I don't understand," I asked Nuada. "What happened?"

"This is some of Hecate's sorcery, I think," he said. "I'm not sure what to make of it."

"Can we open a portal from this place back to the Elysian Fields and bring Cerridwen here?" Nuada asked.

Lucifer shook his head. "No portals can be placed near Mt. Olympus. We opened one as close as we could."

"Then what can we do?" Nuada asked.

"I don't know," he said. "I brought pickaxes and Xia Zeng, the dragon, but I'm afraid of hurting Hecate and Selene. And of releasing Zeus. I'm not sure what is keeping the globe suspended."

"Is there any way to find out if the ball is Hecate's magic or if it belongs to someone else?" I asked.

Lucifer nodded and walked up to it. He touched it gingerly with an ungloved hand. Finally, he said, "It belongs to Hecate."

"Okay, so we know someone else didn't do this. How do we get them out? We can't leave them in there even if we risk releasing Zeus," I said.

"What do you suggest we try first?" asked Nuada.

I touched the ball. It was cold and frozen, but it felt like more than ice. There was magic involved. I closed my eyes and tried to sense what it was.

Lucifer said, "Let's try the pickaxe. See if it has an effect."

I nodded and stepped away. Lucifer took off his pack and pulled out two pickaxes. He kept one and handed one to Anubis.

Lucifer swung at a blank part of the globe, then the dog-headed man swung. They each took several hard whacks at it. It sounded like beating metal pans together, ringing out in the cavern. The ball remained completely unmarked. Not even a crack.

"Stop," I yelled. "It's not having any effect."

Lucifer and Anubis dropped the sledgehammers, exhausted by their effort in the frigid temperature.

"Let's try heat," said Nuada.

Lucifer went to Xia Zeng and whispered a few words to him. The dragon slithered over the globe and opened his mouth. Out came a blue flame which licked the ball, then flattened out and covered a two foot circle. The roaring fire must have lasted a good minute. The dragon paused and did it again. It repeated the effort five times. Lucifer asked it to stop.

The globe was untouched. Lucifer went over and felt the spot which had been flamed and said, "It's not even warm."

Nuada touched it and agreed.

I touched the globe and it turned a light yellow color. I pulled away, frightened.

Lucifer said, "Do that again."

The same thing happened. I knew that I carried Hecate's magic from being infected; the form and the structure of my power came from her. I realized that's why I could affect the globe. It was sealed with her magic.

I imagined the magic heating up the globe and melting it. The ball began to drip and soon there was a puddle of water around my feet. I tried to think of my hand as a match, melting one side of a candle down, where the wax stood higher. Except I was trying to melt a large hole in the globe, not enough to make the whole thing collapse and hurt someone, just enough to release the occupants.

Sweat dripped down my face and made me even colder. I felt my energy level go down, but focused on melting the ice.

It took quite awhile, but finally, I melted a hole large enough that it went all the way through to the center. Lucifer called to Hecate. I could hear them gasping for breath. I think all the oxygen had disappeared. Even goddesses must need to breathe.

I rested for a minute, then pushed Lucifer away and began making the hole larger. It seemed to take forever, but finally, it was large enough to pull Hecate and Selene out.

Lucifer and Nuada lay them on coats on the ground. Then put other coats on top of them, trying to warm them.

"Where is he?" asked Lucifer.

Hecate pointed to the globe.

I went over and peered inside. On the floor was a snake. A very cold snake.

"Seal it," Hecate said.

"I'll try," I said.

I held both my hands up and imagined spraying water onto the globe and cold air freezing it on contact. It took much longer than it did to melt the ball. Eventually, I sealed up the hole and added an extra layer of ice over the entire globe to make it look seamless. While I did this my body cold colder, my teeth began to chatter. I felt as if I would never be warm again.

Hecate said, "Perfect," when I had finished. She was sitting up and drinking warm liquid, which Lucifer must have created. Selene was doing the same.

"What happened?" I asked, shivering. Nuada brought me some hot tea.

Hecate said, "Zeus was able to work a weak spell, even though he'd been changed into a snake. When I tried to encase him in ice, it sealed all of us inside. Selene and I couldn't get out and couldn't call for help. How did you find us?"

"Angelica had a dream," said Lucifer.

Hecate got up and came over to me, hugging me. "How did you die?"

"One of the Furies scratched me as we fled. The venom." I shrugged.

"I am glad we will not lose you at least. But I would have wished for you to live out your normal life on earth."

"Maybe I already did," I said.

"Perhaps you did," she said, sadly, stroking my hair.

When everyone was ready, we left the chamber with the blue ice globe, but first Nuada sealed the doorway, making it look as if it was just another piece of rock wall. Hopefully, that chamber would never be found again.

We made the long trek back to the portal. I felt numb the whole way and stumbled a lot. It was as if I was still back in the cave, staring at the blue globe. Somehow, it didn't seem to take as long to get back as it had to reach our destination.

Then we were back in the solarium. The gloriously warm solarium.

Cerridwen and a group of healers were waiting for us. They took Hecate and Selene to the Healers' room. Lucifer followed. I stumbled to my room and fell on my bed without even undressing.

I was woken by someone pounding on my door.

I groggily got up and opened the door.

Chris stood there looking wild eyed. "What are you doing sleeping at this time of day? You should be celebrating."

"Celebrating what," I managed to mumble.

"Hades and Pluto have surrendered. The war that's been going on for over two thousand years is over!"

I nodded, still deep in my dreams about ice. I kept trying to shake them off, but couldn't.

"You don't look so good," he said.

"I feel awful." I couldn't wake up, no matter how hard I tried.

"Dead people don't get sick. Let's go to the Healers'."

I objected, but he dragged me down the hall.

Nuada was one of the first people I saw. Cerridwen came to me and asked, "What's wrong?"

"Can't wake up. Can't stop dreaming about the journey."

"What journey?" asked Chris.

Cerridwen felt my face. She looked shocked and said, "You are ice cold." She turned to Chris and said, "She went on the journey to rescue Hecate and Selene. Good thing she did, it was only because of Angelica they were found and she's the one who released them. But she's exhausted and needs to rest now. You go along to the celebration. I will take care of her."

Chris looked like he was about to say something, but changed his mind. Cerridwen isn't someone you argue with and win. He left.

Cerridwen exchanged looks with Nuada and said, "We'll get her into a bed and try to get her warm. Then you need to tell me exactly what happened when they were rescued."

I slid into the bed and rolled over, pulling the bedding over my head. I felt relieved to lay down and let go of everything. They kept piling more blankets on. Then they lay their hands on me and I began to get warmer. I drifted off to sleep as Nuada told Cerridwen the story, feeling it happen all over again in my dreams.

Then I heard her say, "She may have caught the edge of Zeus' spell, or she's depleted from using so much powerful magic, or maybe she just absorbed what was floating around in that cave, Hecate's and Zeus' magic."

"What should we do?" asked Nuada.

"Just keep her warm and let her sleep and wait. If she's depleted, she'll fill back up again. If not, then we'll call Hecate."

"I'll stay with her and keep her warm," said Nuada.

As I drifted ever deeper into sleep, Hecate said, "I thought you would."

My dreams kept repeating, over and over. Trapped inside the ice globe. I couldn't get out and I couldn't breathe. Hoar frost formed on the inside of the ball, on my clothes and hair. Then ice froze my skin and I was completely paralyzed and numb.

At one point Hecate touched me and flames chased the ice away, melting it. I heard her say, "Let her sleep. She will be okay now."

Finally, I woke. They wouldn't let me get up though. Apparently I'd been out for a couple of days.

Hecate came to visit and told me what happened.

She said, "When I changed Zeus into the snake, he split off part of himself and put it inside you. Easy to do since you were mortal. He could have controlled you. It must have been very frustrating for him when the Fury attacked you, fatally injuring you. He was then trapped, having made such a dramatic transition with you. He couldn't do much, but he could work on you through dreams."

"He caused the dream that helped us rescue you?" I asked.

"Yes, ironically. His magic may even have assisted in getting us out of the globe. But it wouldn't go into the snake, it couldn't leave your body, without help. So you brought that part of him back with you and it tried to eradicate you."

"Could it have?" I asked.

"Yes. The dead are far from invulnerable. I called a salamander and drew something out of you which looked like white smoke. I blew it into the salamander, binding it there. Then took the salamander, spoke to it in Greek and threw it into the fire on the balcony. The salamander basked in the flames until the piece of Zeus was destroyed, then it vanished into the fire as salamanders are wont to do. You are free of him," she said.

"Thank you."

"I should have noticed it earlier, when I turned him into the snake. I was careless."

"You were preoccupied," I said.

"That may be, but I should have noticed. I'm very sorry you suffered."

"Cerridwen said I'll be all right."

"Yes, you will. But he almost took you. I underestimated him."

"So the war is really over?"

"Yes. I believe Hades and Pluto are actually relieved and looking forward to peace. For a time at least. And I am looking forward to concentrating on something other than defending my people."

I saw Chris come up behind her. I waved at him.

"I shall go and leave you two alone," said Hecate.

Chris sat in the chair beside my bed. I noticed he was grinning so hard, he almost gave off light.

"What?" I asked.

"I came to tell you something that day I woke you up, but you were too sick. I don't even know how to tell you."

"What?"

"Olwen and I are getting married!"

# CHAPTER TWENTY-FOUR

MY MOUTH DROPPED. "You and Olwen, married? I didn't even realize you two were that much of an item!"

"Well, we've all been rather busy. And while the war was on Hecate and Lucifer had a ban on marriages. But I think I fell in love with her when I first saw her sitting by my bedside. Then I noticed she only had one arm and she started helping me deal with the loss of my leg. The more I got to know her, the deeper I fell."

"Congratulations!" I was glad they'd found each other. In real life my brother never had time for romance, he was always too busy with school and sports and being a golden boy.

"It's going to be the same day as several other weddings, the day after tomorrow. Rumor has it that Lucifer and Hecate are getting married too."

"I look forward to seeing that," I said.

"Well, I'll let you rest. I've got to add more bells and whistles to the system today. I just wanted to tell you before someone else did."

"Thanks. Chris, I'm really happy for the two of you."

He turned and practically bounced out of the room.

I sat there in bed feeling lonely. I was the only other person at the Healers' besides Marshall. He was a really old guy who'd been unconscious since long before I first took a shift at the Healers'. There was only one healer on duty, Sarah, and she was out on the balcony, seemingly entranced with what must be wedding preparations. I wondered if I could sneak out and go back to my room. Probably not a good idea.

I rolled over and went to sleep.

I woke to a huge commotion. Five healers were trying to hold down a large, brawny man who was bellowing.

"Get your hands off me. I'm fine I tell you."

Cerridwen swept into the room, then motioned the others away. "Don't you dare move," she said to the guy with a voice which would have immobilized a thrashing elephant.

"Don't order me around, my good woman," he said. I recognized the voice. Arawn. He was covered with blood and had several large, white teeth sticking out of one leg.

"I'm not your woman," she said, icily. "Now, lie still so the healers can do their job."

"It's just a few teeth," he said. "I can get them out."

"Yes, I can see that. I can see what a mess you've made of it already. Now let us do our job or I'll roast your toes and eat them for dinner," she said.

"You wouldn't dare," he boomed.

She got her knife out and motioned for the others to hold him.

"Okay, okay, you old hag. I'll be still."

Cerridwen cut his pant leg off and gradually pulled the teeth out one by one, dropping them into a silver bucket. Arawn moaned and yelled, but didn't move. Cerridwen picked up the bucket and asked, "Who do these belong to?"

"Typhon."

"Typhon? How did you get them?" She asked, setting the bucket down and began washing his wounds.

He started yelling again. In between bursts he managed to gasp out, "I followed Scathach, then left to find Hecate, Angelica and Nuada. I thought I could help, and I know you all didn't trust me, but I needed to prove I was trustworthy. That I could be useful. Nuada was the only one there. With Typhon."

He continued, "I attacked Typhon and when he rocketed into the air, I was hanging on and went with him. What a ride! When he came down I was shaken loose, along with a few of his teeth. One of his dragon headed fingers had latched onto my leg. He took off again and I was left lying there. The poison from the teeth drove me half mad. It took me a while to get my bearings and get back to Lucifer's Lair. Which was nearly empty, except for a few guards. They brought me here."

Cerridwen stood silently touching his leg, then she began mixing herbs. I watched as she returned to his bed and scraped the herbs onto his wounds. He looked instantly relieved. She said, "This will draw the remaining poison, but it looks as if you've transmuted most of it." She wrapped a bandage over the herbs, pointed a finger at him and said, "If I hear that you've given the healers any more trouble or that you've gotten out of bed before I give my okay, I will make good on the offer to roast your toes and eat them!" She glared at him until he nodded.

The she turned and walked away, shook her head and grumbled, "Gods, they're such egotistical idiots."

One of the healers propped a pillow behind his back and asked if she could get him anything. Arawn just waved her off and she quickly retreated from the room. Then he looked around, noticed me and shrugged grumpily as if to say, 'Well what choice do I have?'

I laughed.

He asked, "What are you in here for?"

"Spell gone wrong," I said, "but I'm hoping to get out soon."

"In time for the big nuptials. I overheard the guards talking about it as they brought me in. Long overdue, I'd say. I hope I'm out of here in time to celebrate. It's been far too long since any of us have had cause for such a major celebration."

I nodded, not knowing what to say. I still felt alone. Maybe even more so with him staring at me.

I was all set to slide down into the blankets and pretend to be asleep when Nuada entered the room.

"Good evening everyone," he said in a cheerful voice.

Which somehow made me want to slap him.

He walked to Arawn's bed and said, "Cerridwen tells me I have you to thank for attacking Typhon and chasing him away. I couldn't figure out why he left. I never saw you."

"Well, you wouldn't have. I was invisible. And I couldn't let you sacrifice yourself like that. You've got far too many prospects."

Nuada blushed.

Arawn continued, "And I couldn't have all of you thinking badly of me for eternity. I needed to do something to prove my loyalty to you."

"That was my fault, I'm afraid," said Nuada. "I was the one who didn't trust you."

"Ah well, it's not like I gave you reason to, threatening to try to take away that which you hold most dear." Arawn continued, "But that's all water under the bridge. I never was interested, just harmless fun for an old God."

He seemed anything other than harmless to me. He may have been on our side, but he was still dangerous.

Nuada nodded to him and they did some sort of fancy handshake, some super-powered, Celtic God thing. Nuada moved over near my bed and casually lounged in the chair.

"So, how are you this evening?" he asked.

"I'm okay, I guess. Other than being trapped here. I'd like to go back to my room."

"What would you do there?"

"Crawl under the covers and sleep for a few days."

"I think she's feeling a little let down by her abysmal company," said Arawn.

I didn't say anything.

Nuada said, "You've had a dramatic transformation and more than a little stress. Why wouldn't you feel sad now some of the stress has let up?"

I nodded. If I spoke, I'd probably burst out crying.

He continued, "Our whole world has changed and all of us are scrambling to understand where we fit in it. And you never quite had a place, so it must be even more frustrating for you."

I nodded again.

Nuada sat on the bed and took me into his arms. I began to sob, completely out of control. The more I thought about how embarrassing this was, to break down crying and snotty nosing with the person I wanted to impress the most, the more out of control my sobbing became. He held me and rocked me for the longest time until I ran out of tears and was left with hiccups.

Nuada gave me a drink of water and a handkerchief. Then tucked me in and stroked my hair and face. "You'll see, things will turn out just fine. Give yourself a break and some time to find your place here. I know where your place is," he said.

"Where?"

"Shhhh. Sleep now, we'll talk about it when they release you." He waved his hand in front of my face and I was out.

# CHAPTER TWENTY-FIVE

I WOKE EARLY the next day. Just after breakfast Olwen came to see me.

"I feel like I should come to you and ask permission," she said.

"Why?"

"You are his only kin here. And we haven't been exactly open with what has going on between us. Only Nuada and Lucifer could see it happening. Hecate was too tied up with the war."

"It was quite a surprise to me."

"I really want us to be friends," she said. She reminded me of a sixteen year old girl, rather than a two thousand year old or more, Goddess.

"I think we can be. I understood how it happened, once Chris told me, it was so obvious. But I was shocked. I didn't think gods and mortals, dead or alive, could be lovers, or married."

Olwen looked at me with that sad look I've seen on her face occasionally. "It does happen, more often than one would think. And it doesn't always end happily. Selene was betrayed by her human lover and has not taken a lover since. Although since the war began, there's been little opportunity," she said, studying her hands.

"But there's no rules against it?"

"No, but it is tricky. Those of us with a conscience like to make sure we're not throwing our power around and entrapping defenseless humans."

"Like Zeus."

"Yes," she said, looking at me as if I'd cursed.

"So, it has to be a relationship that's pretty equal," I said.

"Yes, but even then, there is really no way for an affair between a human and a deity to be equal."

"So what does a deity get out of such an unbalanced relationship?" I asked.

"Some gods like the power over another being. Some of us want the novelty of being with a human. Humans, being short lived, are generally more spontaneous and filled with passion. Not so jaded as some of us deities who have lived thousands upon thousands of years," she said.

This world was so complicated and there were so many rules and things I didn't even begin to understand.

I said, "I'm glad you and Chris found each other. He never had time for a girlfriend when he was alive, so he doesn't really know how to do the whole romantic lover thing. You'll have to teach him."

She laughed, her voice sounded like crystal bells. "I welcome a lover who has no pretensions."

Arawn overheard that and howled with laughter, until Cerridwen came in and told him to calm down. Finally, he stopped laughing and with tears streaming from his eyes, said, "It's a good thing you weren't courting me, dear Olwen. I have far too many pretensions."

"And you're far too old for her, you old fart," said Cerridwen, handing him a handkerchief. He blew his nose with a loud snort.

I turned back to Olwen and said, "I wish I could help you or Chris get ready for the wedding. But I'm still in prison."

She said, "Just rest up and get well enough to come. That will be enough."

The next day I was released by Cerridwen. Into Nuada's care.

"Now don't you over do it, young lady," she said. "I don't want to see you in here again as anything except a healer. And I wouldn't want you to miss the weddings. I'll send someone to help you get ready, so go to your room."

Nuada escorted me to my room and waited until Selene came. He said, "I'll be back in three hours after I've changed and helped with the preparations. You are to wait here for me. Do you understand?"

"Yes," I said. I really liked him, but I didn't want a baby sitter. And I didn't think it would take that long to get ready.

I was so very wrong.

Selene was ready, except for her dress. She insisted that I needed to take a scented, luxurious bath and wash my grody hair. Oh, and do the de-hairing of legs and underarms. Then after rubbing scented oils over my body in an awesome massage, Selene braided rosebuds into my hair. Then we painted my finger and toe nails a lovely shell pink. So not my color, but what was my color these days? I had no idea who I was anymore, so I wasn't going to argue about it.

Then there was a little blush, lip color and mascara. She brought me a light pink gown to change into. It was light and flimsy and when I put it on, see through.

"Where's my underwear?" I asked.

"It's summer here. We don't wear underwear."

"I can't go out like this," I said.

She sighed and got me a little white slip thing to wear under the dress. If I didn't raise my arms or bend over, I'd be safe.

Then she helped me strap white sandals on and a delicate necklace of pearls.

She slipped into her dress and put sandals and jewelry on.

I looked at my arm and the raw, red scar from the Fury.

"It won't go away, I'm afraid. The healers tried. It will fade with time," she said.

Soon Nuada knocked on the door.

He wore green pants, sandals and an open vest. A bronze, carved circlet wreathed his bicep and a leather water container was slung over his shoulder. His wavy dark hair fell loose. In short he looked stunning. I almost gasped. I'm sure I gaped. He gave me his arm and led me towards wherever the weddings were at while Selene went off to help Cerridwen gather up Arawn.

We were seated in an open air stadium with stone benches. I wracked my brain for Greek history and finally came up with amphitheatre. That must be what it's called. It sat conveniently in the shade of a massive cliff, so it was somewhat cooler than in the sun. But it felt hot, despite the breeze. Now I knew why they didn't wear clothes. I wouldn't have thought dead people sweated. Shows how much I knew. I waved my hands trying to create a breeze.

Nuada said, "How foolish of me." From the pocket of his vest he pulled out a delicate flowered fan, made of silk.

We were some of the first people there; he'd wanted to get there early enough to get shady seats, because some of them would become really hot as the sun moved across the sky. I'd never realized how many people lived in this section of the Underworld. Some visitors had come from Hades and Pluto's camp as well.

Nuada pointed out a grim looking man, dressed in black whom I recognized as Charon. There were a handful of other Greek gods as well, sitting in the front rows. And maybe Roman, or Cretan or Egyptian. He told me that all the Celtic gods defected early on. Arawn was the last to come, making sure all his people were safe before he came.

There must have been a few thousand people. Musicians began to play string and wind instruments. At first it was really bizarre music that I couldn't place and then it morphed into classical music.

Finally the wedding parties came onto the stage. There were seven couples who were being married. Everyone wore different clothes from their region and era. Poor Chris wore in a tux, he must have been sweating to death.

Every now and then Nuada offered me water from his bag; it tasted lovely, sweet and clean, like all the water here. Even though I felt hot and sweaty, he never broke skin contact with me, which was fine. I wanted to be as close to him as possible. I was absolutely smitten and had been ever since I first saw him as a human. I kind of liked him as a dog too. Those lovely golden eyes.

I concentrated on the stage. Besides Chris and Olwen, Hecate and Lucifer, there was only one other couple I recognized. Godwin and Mabel. They were both healers. I'd had no idea anything was between them other than friendship. They were both so loving and kind. My heart went out to them, thankful that they now had time to be together.

Hecate was dressed all in white and wore white pearls braided into her long hair. Lucifer wore black and seemed to bask in the heat of the sun. Hecate was accompanied by several hounds, snakes and a boar.

A red haired Goddess came out whom Nuada identified as Brighid or Bride, the Celtic Goddess of Fire, Poetry, Smiths and Childbirth. She was dressed in gold and looked like a flame as she took the stage. I'd only seen her in passing, apparently she had lived here, mostly far away from the fighting. She stood in front of everyone and said, "These couples have come before all of us to be wed in the sacred manner with public vows."

She went on for a while; I got lost in the rhythm of her words, the spectacle of colors and costumes and all those people. We drank toasts, although Nuada made me drink water and he drank it too. I heard a low bellow in the row behind me. It was Arawn, Cerridwen was forcing him to drink from a jug in her hand. Her other hand held a small knife. Finally, he relented and drank water for a toast. When he finished I noticed he was smiling, although hiding it from her. He really seemed to enjoy baiting her and she was having none of it.

Then the couples each repeated vows. The sun was beginning to hit the bleachers. Most of the people seemed to be having no problem with the heat. I was wilting and seriously considering stripping and dumping the contents of Nuada's water bag over my head.

I leaned against Nuada and he immediately summoned a cool breeze to blow on me. "I'm sorry," he said. "I didn't think the heat would bother you so much. This part will be over soon and we can find a place for you to cool off."

The breeze felt wonderful and invigorating. I watched as the couples exchanged rings and repeated more vows. Then they kissed. That seemed to be the end of the formal part of the wedding. They left the stage and very slowly the rest of us filed out.

Everyone else was going down to exit, but Nuada took me up and we went out a back way, into some rock caverns. They were dark and cool. He felt my head and said, "Lie down on the floor, with your face on the rock."

"Why?"

"You need to cool off before we leave. And that will give the crowds time to thin out."

"I'll get all dirty." I didn't want to ruin this lovely dress.

"Our next stop will be the fountains," he said.

I lay down on the floor of the cavern, feeling the overwhelming heat sink into the smooth floor. It felt like polished stone. He sat beside me, leaning against a stone wall.

"I've been meaning to talk to you, but I can't ever seem to see you when you're conscious and alone. A difficult combination."

"What about?" I asked, my words echoing off the stone floor. I turned my head in his direction.

"You know I'm in love with you," he said.

"No, I didn't know." I just lay there, but at the same time the girl in my head was jumping up and down screaming!

"Well, I am. I fell in love with you the first instant I saw you, when I was a dog. Hecate knew. I had annoyed her, so part of the reason she assigned me to you was to get back at me, make me suffer because I knew I could never have you."

"Why?" I asked.

"A thousand reasons. We were at war and no couplings were allowed, you were alive and I'm immortal. I was your caretaker and I couldn't take advantage of you. There were oh, so many reasons."

"And now?"

"Now you are dead. The war is over. She and Lucifer allowed your dead brother and Olwen to marry. There is hope they will allow us to marry."

"Is that a proposal?" I asked. Stupid question. I was stalling, worried about everything which could go wrong. Why couldn't I ever just be happy?

"Yes. Angelica, could you love me? Will you marry me and stay with me for all eternity?"

"I don't know. Don't get me wrong. I love you. I just don't understand how a romantic relationship can work between a god and a human, I mean really work. My parents couldn't make it with just two humans. And all eternity is a very long time. And I don't even know you. Not really. Even though I love you."

He gazed at me thoughtfully, "Well, perhaps we could marry as my people did. For a year and a day. With the option of renewing our vows in a year when they expire. At some point you might choose to reincarnate. You lived such a short time on Earth."

I lay on the cool floor, my heart flushed with emotion. "Yes. That I could do. I have no idea what the future might bring."

He rolled me over and kissed me, his skin cool.

"Come," he said. "Let us go play in the fountains while the others start eating and drinking. You are still overheated."

We made our way down the stone steps and into the garden in front of the main building. Tables of food and drink were set up everywhere. The feast had begun. I just wanted to be alone with Nuada. We went around to the side and found a place in the garden empty of people, but filled with water. A long trough which jetted fountains ten feet into the air, lay in front of us. I took off my sandals and waded into the knee deep water. Nuada removed his shoes, drinking bag and vest, then followed me. It didn't take long before we were drenched. And I was finally cool enough. Although I thought my heart might burst, it felt so full. I couldn't stop smiling.

We romped and played and splashed water at each other, eventually joined by several other people, including a very drunk Arawn and his keeper, Cerridwen. She winked at me as she pushed him flat on his back in the water. He yelled and yanked on her leg until she lost her balance and joined him. Then they each had another drink or two from her drinking bag, which I gathered was now filled with wine.

Finally, Nuada and I got out, gathered up our things and went in search of food.

He asked me, "When would you like to tell people the news?"

I thought for a moment as I chewed on a lovely hunk of meat, "Tomorrow, or the next day. Let the couples who got married tonight have their time to celebrate."

He nodded, smiling.

I worried a little about how we'd get on together, he had been around a couple thousand years longer than me, but I knew it would be okay.

We had all the time in the universe to get it figured out.

---

IF YOU'RE LOOKING for another good read, check out *The Jeweled Worlds Series.*

*The Black Opal: The Jeweled Worlds Series, Book 1*
(This trilogy is now complete with Book 3)

# ABOUT THE AUTHOR

LINDA JORDAN writes fascinating characters, visionary worlds, and imaginative fiction. She creates both long and short fiction, serious and silly. She believes in the power of healing and transformation, and many of her stories follow those themes.

In a previous lifetime, Linda coordinated the Clarion West Writers' Workshop as well as the Reading Series. She spent four years as Chair of the Board of Directors during Clarion West's formative period. She's also worked as a travel agent, a baker, and a pond plant/fish sales person, you know, the sort of things one does as a writer.

Currently, she's the Programming Director for the Writers Cooperative of the Pacific Northwest.

Linda now lives in the rainy wilds of Washington state with her husband, daughter, four cats, a cluster of Koi and an infinite number of slugs and snails.

Her other work includes:

- *The Black Opal: Jeweled Worlds Series, Book 1*
- *The Enigmatic Pearl: Jeweled Worlds Series, Book 2*
- *The Flaming Ruby: Jeweled Worlds Series, Book 3*
- *Faerie Unraveled: The Bones of the Earth, Book 1*

All her work can be found at your favorite online bookseller.

Get a FREE ebook!
Sign up for Linda's Serendipitous Newsletter at her website:
www.LindaJordan.net
She can be found on Facebook at:
www.facebook.com/LindaJordanWriter
Metamorphosis Press website is at:
www.MetamorphosisPress.com
Goodreads: https://www.goodreads.com/author/show/
2021274.Linda_Jordan

Writers love reviews, even short, simple ones. Please go to where you bought this book, or Goodreads, and leave a review. It would be much appreciated.